Coast Lines

stories and poems from

West Sussex Writers

2017

Copyright

Copyright © 2017 by The Authors

The moral rights of the listed authors to be identified as the authors of this work has been asserted by them in accordance with the Copyright, Designs and Patents Act 1988.
All the characters in this book are fictitious, and any resemblance to actual persons living or dead is purely coincidental.

All rights reserved.

This book or any portion thereof may not be reproduced or used in any manner whatsoever without the express written permission of the authors except for the use of brief quotations in a book review.

Edited by Phil Williams
Published by Rumian Publishing

ISBN: 978-0-9931808-2-8

Contents

PART ONE – WORDS FROM THE CHAIRS

PART TWO - PROSE

Spectacular Flights of Whales 6
Susanne Conboy-Hill

Raptor 12
Jackie Harvey

A Cushy Number 14
Terence Brand

Never Too Old 20
Sue Ajax-Lewis

Mavis and the Microwave 21
Lela Tredwell

Hank's Last Flight 27
Andrew Westgate

for better for worse... 31
Paul Doran

Tripping up Chanctonbury Ring 32
Patricia Graham

Blue Bell Hill 37
Nina Tucknott

Fulfilling the Dream 42
Rose Bray

The Ring 44
Janet Rogers

Of Goats and Gigabytes 49
Phil Williams

God Bless Gary 54
Cherrie Taylor

The Feathering of Peacocks 55
Audrey Lee

The Here and Now 59
Pat Hopper

My Name is Tony 64
Ian C. Black

The Old Canal 69
Alison Batcock

The Elastic Heart 71
Alison Hawes

...but the stars started to disappear 74
Caroline Collingridge

The Possibilities are Endless 76
Kathy Schilbach

The Turqoise Ring 77
Cherrie Taylor

Trekking with the Toads 80
Christine Mustchin

Today 87
Sandra Wood-Jones

We Never Knew 88
Rhona Gorringe

Mermaid 93
Audrey Lee

The Gardens 98
Cherrie Taylor

A Dog Named Useless 99
Patricia Feinberg Stoner

Can Buy Me Love 104
Sue Ajax-Lewis

Our Best Friend Buster 109
John Falconer

PART THREE - POETRY

Have you ever... 114
Lyn C. Jennings

Raising the Bowman 116
Rose Bray

It's Not Cricket, It's a Scorpion 117
Dave Simpson

It Couldn't Happen Here... 118
Cherrie Taylor

Scarecrows 120
Derek Eastwoord

Muscovies 121
Richard Buxton

Three Seasons of War in Four Trios 123
Liz Eastwood

Terzanelle - A Windswept Soul 125
Terry Westwood

Pebble 126
Audrey Lee

I Wish I'd Married A Billionaire 127
Cherrie Taylor

My Son, Our Boy 128
Paul Doran

Daddy's Gone 129
Alexander Medwell

Cross Rail Dig 131
Lyn C. Jennings

Nineteen Forty-Five 133
Audrey Lee

To Alex Peckham 135
Audrey Lee

Homefield Park 137
Laurie Morris

The Monthly Test 138
Dave Simpson

Miscarriage 140
Alison Batcock

A Prayer for the World in 2017 for All Faiths 141
Caroline Collingridge

Seven-Seven 142
Wendy Green

PART FOUR – BIOGRAPHIES

PART ONE

WORDS FROM THE CHAIRS

There's a really special thing about going into a bookshop or even (crikey) a supermarket, and seeing books by people you know on the shelves. Yes, we've had quite a few well-known (and not so well-known) names come and talk to us at West Sussex Writers over the years and it's good to recognise them, or hear them mentioned on the radio, or see one of their plays or films… But the real excitement comes from meeting people in a drafty hall somewhere, knowing they've been looking for an agent, or a publisher, for years and thankless years and then, bang, there they are on the 3 for 2 tables, or being performed at the Fringe.

Of course, not everyone can be a Jan Henley, Rosanna Ley, Sophie Duffy, Pam Weaver, Sarah Higbee, Alison Hawes, Stella Whitelaw etc etc… And that's what's great about West Sussex Writers. Anyone, no matter how many titles they've had published - or not - or number of words they've written this week - or not - is welcomed, encouraged, supported.

I was really proud to chair West Sussex Writers for several years, and previously to work on the committee when Wendy Green and Nina Tucknott were Chairs. We were a tight-knit group for my three years as Chair, and our committee meetings were always fun and filled with cheese - even if we never did all manage to get to Heather's without phoning for assistance at least once.

I've got to say that running fast and loose with the day-glo orange heating system at Heene Gallery (as was) is amongst my fondest memories of my time as Chair, along with Alison Hawes' cakes, mulled wine for the masses and banning American Tan tights from the raffle table.

If I had to pick one meeting, though, it would have to be the screening of Laurie Morris's film which was produced by the South Downs Film Club, the prize for winning a screen-writing competition devised by the redoubtable Godfreys. There was such a buzz in the Gallery that night, which for me epitomised everything West Sussex Writers stands for. Plus, it was a great film!

This anthology is a great way to celebrate the success of West Sussex Writers, and to showcase the talent that exists within the group. It's no surprise WSW has lasted as long as it has, and long may it continue.

Sarah Palmer
Chair, West Sussex Writers, 2011-2015

The lady mayor and the punk poet. Together. What could possibly go wrong?

It was the 60th anniversary of the West Sussex Writers' Club and Day For Writers at Durrington College. The day had not begun well. It was an early Saturday start for all, particularly the organisers and especially if you lived in Horsham as I did and do. One arrival, having been down the previous evening to set up, we found that our helpful contact had been suspended for an unspecified disciplinary offence. Naturally neither he nor the college had mentioned this to us on the Friday evening. So it was do-it-yourself time.

Then the lady mayor of Worthing – a writer of poetry herself – was giving the opening welcome speech. Of one of our tutors, famed punk poet Attila The Stockbroker (influences Hilaire Belloc and The Clash) no sign. There soon was. As the dear lady continued her gracious and polite speech, into the hall came noisily and belatedly our man in leather jacket, jeans and boots. He took a pew in the second row and threw his boots up on the vacant chair in the row in front. I cringed inwardly. What sort of disaster was this day going to be?

None. We had a very successful Diamond Day For Writers. As to Attila, whose workshop I attended as a poet, he turned out to be a brilliant – first-time - tutor, encouraging, positive and quite a coup for the Club – if of course not to everybody's taste. Most of his ire was reserved for a literary agent who said she "didn't deal with literary fiction or poetry" (commercially reasonable, probably – though I would question the first – and there are no agents in poetry, as there's no money). As someone who had started and kept his own career as performance poet going himself, Attila had no time for this.

When I think back to my time as Chairman of West Sussex Writers' Club – which has rightly now lost the man and the Club, although most of the Chairmen were anyway female – what I recall is friendship, talent and the most efficient committees I have ever come across. We worked together, we got things done and we worked well. Observably this has continued. As writers we had varying degrees of success and fame, but I can't recall any serious animosity – which was good because obviously a lot of people were keen to win the competitions… My other roles in the Club were Competition Secretary (pre-Chair) and Auditor (after), the latter a bit over-praised for an annual task which my Treasurers made simple by their efficiency. I also contributed "From Pen to

Processor: A History of the WSWC", sold for funds, to the Club's 60th and helped to get a Lottery grant.

In my time the Club met mostly at Heene Road Community Centre, which was an acoustically good and easily manageable space. We met – and had in the Club – a number of notable and prominent authors – and others. We had a very popular meeting for crime authors addressed by a policeman. He asked me beforehand – and I thanked him for doing so – whether to play a tape of a woman being murdered. My reply was "They're writers, let them use their imagination." I could see complaints coming but really it was simpler than that – the notion made me queasy.

It is startling that this is so long ago – and yet not. Our stalwart Day For Writers organiser Ian Mallender, a great guy and friend to whom I dedicate this, became a Parkinson's sufferer and died a few years back. Some of the people I knew are still involved, others less so. I have attended less in recent years, in part after repeated advice to use "social" media for which I have, in both senses, no time. There is still a day job and family responsibilities, but the .... (formerly Club) is still in my heart. In fact, last night I came across and played my contribution – and others' – to the 70th anniversary CD "70 Not Out". It is no small thing to me to have my words – which I had almost forgotten about – read by the talented and indefatigable supporter Simon Brett – in a Canadian accent.

Happy 80th to West Sussex Writers! You've done the difficult bit – now the centenary looms…

Anyway stop reading this now. As an old friend and sometime member said (from her writing course): "Have you been to the page today?"

Lawrence Long
Chairman, West Sussex Writers, 1997-2000

PART TWO

PROSE

Spectacular Flights of Whales

Susanne Conboy-Hill

Her: Can fish fly?
Him: Flying fish can.
Her: No, I mean proper flying, like over cities and things because...
Him: You gone soft in the head or something?
Her: ...Because there's one going round your chimney.

Whether it was the beginning of the end, the end of the beginning, or something else entirely turned out to be immaterial. After a short interlude during which astronomers reported a slight increase in background radiation and sunsets appeared rather more purple than usual, the sky turned green and filled up with fish.

To start with, it was mostly shoals of minnows and sardines wheeling and flashing in the sky, or following the main roads way above the traffic like they'd been drawn closer by the air currents. Then it was brown carp, sand dollars, and sea urchins dotting the sky like pin pricks, or dipping down over high rise buildings and getting caught up in the whorls and eddies there before powering off back above the clouds.

Naturally, the major religions sought either to lay blame or to make claim, based on their default positions regarding divine retribution. To whit: who most deserved to cop it for having a rap sheet going all the way back to the Neanderthals, and who could expect to bathe in eternal glory having consistently laid out sets of idiosyncratically derived items in front of equally idiosyncratically derived shrines. Some consequently drew in congregations of glass-half-empties with doom-laden notions of the End of Days, while others garnered the happy-clappies by promoting the more cheery notion of cosmic rebirth; both of which, as it turned out, had some currency.

Science, in the meantime, kept its collective head down while trawling for answers, hypotheses, or anything in fact that would sound convincing and not like the script of a Japanese cartoon where the sushi was about to get its own back. In the interim it had to fend off strident accusations regarding covert experiments with antimatter at the Large Hadron Collider and suggestions that Hubble was back-projecting the population of a wholly aquatic world from the other side of the galaxy.

Him: Quantum entanglement, I betcha.
Her: So that's what happened to string theory – the cats finally burst out of the internet, took over the universe and tied it in knots!
Him: Ok, so explain me all the fish.

Wildlife experts opted out entirely from the awkward explanatories and went with descriptive ethology instead as it was easier on the brain and also made better telly. The fish were very obliging – swirling in vast silvery murmurations high above cities and deserts alike; and people followed them, alerted by a new breed of Shoal-Chasers in large vehicles with satellite dishes on the top. Some speculated with indecent curiosity on what would happen if a particularly large shoal were to meet a particularly large tornado, but of course this had very little currency as there wouldn't be any more tornadoes. The flights of whales, when they came, were spectacular. Huge creatures the colour of bruises that rolled through the air like silent thunder, accompanied by the roseate flashings of a myriad fleeing krill. RTAs increased, A&E departments filled up with victims of careless perambulation, and a few unfortunates walked off cliffs due to the novel but completely understandable attention deficit disorder.

But quite soon, people stopped bumping into each other or smacking into lampposts and began looking where they were going again, and as nothing untoward seemed to come of the phenomenon, enterprise set about finding ways of monetising it. Big business preemptively drew up fishing rights and projected strings of seafood restaurant franchises, while small start-ups worked on developing new technologies such as apps that would predict where the nearest aerial display could be found, to the annoyance of the Shoal-Chasers who had developed their own technology, and added a fair amount of redundant but theatrical bravado to spice up their role. Conversely, the gaming industry abandoned screen apps and went boldly for a revolutionary new goldfish bowl headset design plus wearable fins for zapping targets, the hordes of enthusiasts providing diversionary amusement or minor annoyance by bursting into shops shouting, "Guppy!" Calls of "Viviparous eelpout!" on the other hand, could result in an AR twitcher stampede as these carried maximum points, so it was wise to have some knowledge of ichthyological taxonomy handy.

Unsurprisingly, coteries of enthusiastic movie directors, spotting opportunities for high-end visuals without need of expensive CGI units, got going on dramatisations ranging in style from the Kafka-esque, which nobody understood any better than the reality, to predictable epics featuring an archetypal hero stoically but amusingly risking life and limb to meet the creatures aloft and bring back the message that only humanity could save them. This narrative had no currency at all.

As more new species appeared, many of the smaller varieties began seeping further and further into the lower atmosphere to occupy street-level spaces; forming halos that danced around people's faces and shimmered above their coffees, quite unexpectedly boosting the market for 3D TVs. So many were there that they began to block out the sun despite being intangible – a fact determined by a sky diver who made it his mission to jump onto the back of an orca. With his eyes shut and his parachute open, he braced himself for landing only to find himself still travelling downwards with nothing but a vague feeling of internal molecular discombobulation to report at the end.

Him: Told you, holograms.
Her: From where?
Him: You wait, it's Moore's Law and something really big's coming.

It was. One Saturday afternoon the thrashing tail of a sperm whale took the top off The Shard in London and the air was suddenly full of falling debris and raucous sirens. The media went into a meltdown of recrimination over whose fault it was that no one had seen this coming, and a plethora of badly-phrased petitions appeared demanding a government debate about it.

It was a game-changer and caused a groundswell of unease, even though it had happened at a weekend when there had not been full occupancy and there were only two fatalities. What had been insubstantial had become undeniably less so and was therefore no longer an entertainment but an obvious Health and

Safety risk which had to be put a stop to. There was also now the problem of waste disposal which, in the case of whales, was not inconsiderable. On the plus side, sales of golf umbrellas rocketed.

Her: Your hologram just pooped on the Palace garden party.
Him: Didn't it just – splatt-er-ooo!
Her: Shouldn't laugh...
Him: Prince Philip though...

Also not inconsiderable was the next group of fish to arrive. Deep sea denizens, ugly as sin and prone to dangle their lures anywhere small creatures might be found. Kittens, baby squirrels and meerkats of any age were most vulnerable because they were unfailingly drawn to the dangling doo-dad, and the internet was soon full of vimeos featuring cute animals pursued by or beating the bejabbers out of, gross predators with cavernous mouths that left little room for a brain. The smaller ones, that was. The larger gross predators were even more alarming to look at and so, dubbed Hell's Angel Fish and forming the inspiration for cartoons featuring humpback anglers on amphibious bikes, they were largely left to their own devices. Being ponderously passive hunters, they actually only managed to snare drunks and adrenaline junkies, which seemed something of a public service.

Further unease bordering on slight panic came as the expansion of species in both numbers and locations accelerated. Aquatic life appeared deep in the mines and places where scientists were trying to trap neutrons; interfering with machinery by growing on it, dissolving it, absorbing it, and spitting bits of it out in useless molecular configurations. And passengers off on holiday in high flying jets began to find clown fish and muddy-looking sticklebacks in their drinks. Everyone wanted a Nemo, apart from small boys who almost universally coveted the Blob Fish, and people pretended to drink them while taking selfies. This practice halted with the advent of piranhas, at which point a class action suit was taken out against a major airline company.

Politicians variously blamed other countries, denied they had a problem, or tried to sell the whole shebang as a unique tourist attraction before finally recognising the basic Gestalt of their situation – that the whole was very definitely greater than the sum of its parts and that its parts were no longer confined either to their particular patch of sky or even to the sub-troposphere but included actual space. North Korea claimed to have had its suspiciously unannounced moon lander, which it said was equipped with nuclear missiles pointed directly at the West, knocked off course by a school of porpoise, which it further claimed were quite obviously American. This was dismissed as egomaniacal bandwagoning, although the porpoise thing sounded about right. But then a coterie of jellyfish, part of a large bloom orbiting in the same plane, was spotted bobbing about next to the International Space Station. The astronauts had already reported that their docking hatch was occupied by a large Grouper and did Houston have any ideas for shifting it?

A net, Houston? Why would we have a net?

You want us to break out the planaria experiment and hang them on the end of the payload arm? Because why, Houston?

They're worms and it's a fish? You all city boys down there, Houston?

Speculation as to why all this was happening (the *how* would have come further down the line had there been time) ran from a collision of mirror universes, through disturbances in cosmological dark matter, to Pisces getting stuck in the ascendant due to Pluto's confusion about its status as a planet. Some proposed it to be a bit of fancy footwork devised by Google to market its next generation of augmented reality wearables, and Facebook began to run ads for goggles based on poorly-spelled searches.

But they were all way off track, as evidenced by the emergence of a supposedly mythical leviathan from the Mariana Trench at such force that it reached escape velocity without ever troubling a city's skyline. Unfortunately, there was no time then for the kind of moment the film industry had led people to believe they might have at the end of the world - not revenge, not a wild time in a casino, not even a cryptic quip - because it involved the earth demagnetising its core, cracking open its crust, and discharging a large volume of green fluid into earth orbit. The earth then collapsed in on itself, giving rise to a starless gap resembling a sink hole down which the returning tidal flow began to drain. Any interested observers would have been intrigued to see that it did not swirl to the left or to the right, just plunged on through, behaving more like a broken drainpipe than a plug hole. As it did so, taking with it anything that had so far survived, which was mostly the brainless doo-dad danglers and those maggotty shrimps that hang out around deep sea fumeroles, a small creature – astronomically speaking – unfurled itself in the newly created space and announced its arrival with a massive multi-spectrum burp. An answering call from the Crab Nebula would eventually cause a scientist on Tau Ceti C (not their name for it, obviously, but even Klingon doesn't come close) to write *Wow!* for a second time on his computer printout, before nipping outside to see if any more peculiar stuff had shown up in the sky since his shift started.

Raptor

Jackie Harvey

The tree was bare, snaking branches outlined against the sky, so I could clearly see the figure hunched on the snagging bough. But waiting for what? There was nothing around only dying vegetation, fallen leaves and the smell of damp earth. I half closed my eyes, trying to focus on the figure. *Did it move or was it just the wind winding itself through the wood?* From above, the sound of mewing buzzards filled the air as they circled on the thermals.

Yes, I'm sure the figure moved. It's changed shape, bigger now. Beside me Bess, my Labrador, also sensed my awareness. She sat by my side, nose working overtime at the scents and smells surrounding her. The sound of distant gun-fire was proof of a pheasant shoot deeper into the wood. The figure on the bough moved again, further along the branch.

The dappled sunlight danced amongst the trees as Bess and I moved nearer. Then she froze. I did the same. A snap of twigs in the undergrowth from behind stalled us. Bess growled as two figures trudged towards us. Dressed in waxed coats Adan Welles they carried ruck-sacks and a large net.

The older man spoke quietly, "Sorry to disturb you, just wondered whether you'd seen anything unusual?"

I pointed to the figure on the bough. "Could it be that?"

He looked skyward. "Ah yes, looks like Rosie alright." He turned to his colleague. "Better get the gear out, Bob."

Holding out a lure, Bob whistled up to the figure. It moved further along the bough. He whistled again. The bough sprang into life as Rosie took flight and soared towards us. Her wings darkened the sky as she grew nearer. Bob stood still, arm extended as Rosie landed, her powerful talons engulfing the out-held meat. Her vast wing span, hooked beak and penetrating eye were terrifying but beautiful.

"Good girl," Bob said quietly. He turned to me and Bess. "Meet Rosie our Golden Eagle, she's been missing from the Bird of Prey Sanctuary for three weeks." He stroked her head, "We've had reports of sightings but it's a huge relief to have her back."

I gazed at Rosie in awe and Bess growled. Then we watched as Rosie was carefully secured on Bob's arm and taken back through the wood to safety.

A Cushy Number

Terence Brand

I flew into RAF Changi, Singapore, on a moonlit April evening in 1961. After twenty-one hours cooped up with a score of squabbling RAF families, I desperately needed fresh air. Stepping eagerly onto the aircraft's gangway, I took a deep breath – and choked. You can cut Singapore's atmosphere with a knife. Even at nine in the evening humidity tops ninety percent.

After spending a restless night sharing a hut with a tribe of lively cockroaches, I reported to the Station Warrant Officer's headquarters to collect my blue ticket. Still itching with revulsion, I bent the admin sergeant's ear. "That vermin infested transit billet should be condemned, Sarge. It's bloody disgusting."

He glared at me. I shut up. Sergeants don't forget bolshie airmen.

I spent my first day on Changi carrying my blue ticket to every far-flung corner of the camp. My particulars were noted in the Guardhouse by a point-device RAF policeman; in the Station Post Office a long-suffering corporal suggested I report back when I'd been billeted; a resplendent Clothing Store clerk eyed me from top to toe as if measuring me for a coffin; a fat cook of unknown rank wearing blue and white checked trousers and a soup-stained jacket added me to his meals roster – and so on and so on.

Eventually I came, sweaty and tired, to the window of Technical Wing Disciplinary and Manning Control. Here I would be assigned living quarters and a place of work. I handed my ticket to the clerk sitting in the window. A tall, slim, dark-haired Flight Sergeant stood behind him.

The clerk pored over my ticket. "Bloody hell," he said, looking up at the Flight Sergeant. "Another engine mechanic, Chief – they're coming out of our ears."

"Send him down to 205 Squadron."

"Okay, Chief. And I'll billet him in Block 151."

I put my head into the window. "Er, Chief? 205 is Shackletons isn't it?"

"Something wrong with Shackletons, lad?"
"Piston engines, Chief – I'm jets."
"Is that a fact? You'd better go to Aircraft Servicing Flight then."

The ASF hangers also had engine mechs 'coming out of their ears'. My first week on Changi saw me learning several new card games and smoking far too many cheap cigarettes. The corporals and sergeants consistently called upon their favourites to assist them; being the last to arrive, I languished in the crew room, bored to tears.

Out of desperation I began to help the airframe mechs. One morning I was squatting high on a Hastings' mainplane, laboriously screwing down panels when a corporal shouted across the hanger, "Anyone want to work in an office for a fortnight? The clerk's been posted."

I leapt to my feet. "That'll do me, Corps," I yelled. "Point me at this office."

'This office' turned out to be Technical Wing Disciplinary and Manning Control. The Yorkshire Flight Sergeant who had sent me to ASF greeted me with a frown. "You're not a clerk," he said. "You're an engine mech, jets. I need a clerk."

"Sorry, Chief," I said. "I'm what you're getting. But don't panic – an engine mech's worth a dozen clerks." The Flight Sergeant's frown deepened. "Present company excepted," I added quickly.

It turned out that Flight Sergeant Don Ellison had not been on the island much longer than me. He'd had to pick up the office's duties from Dickson, the clerk who'd been snatched from him by the inconsiderate Station Warrant Officer; or, more likely, his unsympathetic sergeant.

Even more typical of bumbling RAF organisation, the Wing's adjutant, Warrant Officer Pocket, had been at his desk next door for less than a month. Talk about new brooms sweeping clean – none of us knew where the dirt was, did we?

It soon became apparent that my new chief was unwell. Once I had taken my seat in the window, he left me to my own devices. I spent several lonely days figuring out the wall graphs and filing systems. One morning Mr Pocket slid back the hatch in the wall and saw I'd moved to Chiefy's desk. He asked, "Where's the

Flight Sergeant?"

I continued to rummage through Chiefy's files. "He's gone sick, sir."

Mr Pocket nodded. "Even so, I'm not sure those are for your eyes, Newton."

"Ordinarily I'd agree with you, sir. But the Station Post Office wanted an answer yesterday and if they're to get it tomorrow I need to know it now."

The hatch closed on Mr Pocket's bewildered expression. Nothing more was said about my takeover of Chiefy Ellison's big, comfortable chair.

A day or two later, I arrived in the office to find Chiefy Ellison sat at his desk, going through the current files. "Morning, Chief," I said. "Good to see you. The MO sorted you out, has he?"

He shook his head. "I'm not sure, lad. He says I've to drink six extra pints of fluid a day. I asked him if beer would do and he said yes."

"Gawd! Did you tell him you already drink six pints of Tiger of an evening?"

"I hadn't the heart." He stared at a chart on the wall. "I don't know how I'm going to manage it."

I grinned at him. "You'll do it, Chief – I've every faith in you."

He smiled. "I expect you're right, lad."

We soon returned to the old routine, Mr Pocket and I. While Chiefy diligently pursued his cure, I handled his and my work well enough to gain the Adjutant's confidence. My fortnight's reprieve stretched to a month. There were problems in the offing: the Air Officer Commanding was doing his rounds of Far Eastern Command; Changi's A.O.C.'s Parade promised a deal of unaccustomed work - hopefully Chiefy would be fit by then - but otherwise I had surfaced in a potential sewer sucking a Mars bar.

I settled into a pleasant daily schedule: breakfast at nine in the Variety Club's café; an hour and a half for lunch; finish for the day at around 4.30pm. I was set to complete my tour masquerading as Tech Wing's General Clerk in my cool office; the steamy, oily hanger I had gratefully escaped all but forgotten.

The Station Warrant Officer's sergeant had different ideas, however. One bright morning there appeared, among a batch of new arrivals waving their blue chits under my nose, a small individual, moving stiffly in heavily starched Khaki Drill shorts.

This individual purported to be an admin wallah, sent to Technical Wing Disciplinary and Manning Control to fill the established position of General Clerk, which, the SWO's office's records suggested, had been empty for several weeks.

Shakily, I read the sergeant's instructions for a second time. My cushy little number was up. I was to go back to the hanger, back to grease and grit, all-seeing sergeants and crafty corporals. Back to that sad crewroom. Back to endless card schools, played with packs that shuffled like blankets.

I wiped a bead of sweat from an eye. Bugger that, I wasn't going without a fight. "No vacancy for a clerk here," I said. I looked at my watch. "The SWO's office is closed. Go back in the morning. Bags of work for clerks on Admin Wing."

With a look of relief, the little fellow took his ticket and scuttled off. He hadn't relished working on Tech Wing any more than I had of going back to the hanger.

His relief wasn't mutual. I doubted that the SWO's sergeant knew that an engine mech had usurped the position of Technical Wing's General Clerk; more likely he was acting on a subordinate's report of a vacancy that needed filling. Whatever, it boiled down to the same thing – he was on my case. When the little admin wallah claimed Tech Wing had chucked him back, the sergeant would want to know why his office's records were seemingly incorrect.

All that night I ruminated on the fate soon to befall me. Could I stop, or even delay for a week or two, the SWO's sergeant's next attempt to furnish Tech Wing with its missing clerk? Even better, could I devise a plan to convince him that there was no vacancy to fill?

Did he and I rely on the same means to show vacancies? Tech Wing Discip's wall charts were prime examples of the RAF's traditional method of keeping track of its personnel. Presumably, the SWO's sergeant would depend on similar charts. Kept up to date by his clerks, of course.

My charts consisted of indications of the staff a section was entitled to—the Establishment - with a gap beside each figure into which I marked the number of personnel the section could muster presently. A sheet of Perspex laid over the chart allowed me to make the mark with a chinagraph pencil. That way, as airmen came or went, I could rub out the figure and update it. I tried to picture the walls of the SWO's office. I couldn't remember – did the sergeant rely on the same system?

The SWO's office opened at 8am. The next morning I crawled from my pit at an unearthly hour, washed, shaved, donned my best KD and cycled to Admin Wing. At two minutes past eight, I looked through the office's big window. No sergeant – just a single clerk on the telephone. I stepped inside. The clerk covered his mouthpiece. "Be with you in a tick."

"No rush," I said, forcing a smile.

I looked around. Yes! There, on the opposite wall, above the filing cabinets – a set of familiar charts. God – there were about ten of them. Which one was us?

Sidling across the floor, trying to look casual, I read the title at the head of each board. Pay Section, Accounts, Cookhouse, Station Post Office – what about Tech Wing? There – that's it!

I scanned the shining Perspex. Where the hell was Tech Wing Discip? It must be there. Wait! Manning Control – they had it under Manning Control.

And its box was marked with a big black zero.

The clerk had his back to me, phone to an ear. I pulled a bunch of chinagraph pencils from a top pocket. Selecting the black one, I turned to the chart.

"Morning, airman – what can we do for you at this early hour?"

I swung round to come face to face with the dreaded sergeant. "Morning, Sarge," I stammered, hiding my pencils behind my back. "I don't want to bother you. A quick word with your clerk will do – when he comes off the phone."

"That's all right, son. You can tell me. What's your problem?"

My problem was him, but I couldn't tell him that. My brain went blank.

The sergeant studied me. "Don't I know you, son?"

I shook my head. Seeing that the clerk was holding the phone to his chest and looking at us, I said thankfully, "I think you're wanted, Sarge."

As he turned away, I licked my thumb, swept it across the fateful zero, made a swift stroke with my pencil and, stuffing it and the rest of my pencils into my pocket, practically ran for the door. Calling, "I'll come back when you're not so busy," I let myself out of the office, got on my bike and pedalled unsteadily away. Glancing back through the glass, I saw that both men were leaning over the phone. Neither showed the slightest interest in an idiot airman. With luck, later that morning, when the new arrival reported back to the clerk, the clerk would check his graph and think he'd misread it the day before.

Chiefy was putting down the phone as I arrived, still perspiring freely, at Tech Wing Discip. "That was the SWO's office," he said. "Sergeant Rushton."

I gazed at him, the sweat running down my back suddenly cold. So much for luck – the gloomy hanger beckoned. I croaked, "Oh, yes?"

"Aye. Mike says if you're that keen on the job, you'd better keep it."

Never Too Old

Sue Ajax-Lewis

Mrs. Nettle hobbled slowly. The shop must be here somewhere but all the dust and grime on the windows and her failing eyesight made it difficult to see. There it was. She stopped; her heart beating fast. Never had she thought she would have to visit such shabby surroundings. Inside, she quailed as the stubbly grubbily unwashed man looked her over.

"Blimey Gran, you in the right place?"

"Bet yer daren't," Bert had jeered at their weekly pensioners meeting. She would show him! Mrs. Nettle squared her shoulders and lifted her chin.

"Yes," she said firmly, "I want a tattoo."

Mavis and the Microwave

Lela Tredwell

It was three months after Harold died that the microwave started to be abusive.

Mavis told this to the repairman, who merely shrugged.

"Do you think that means anything?" she asked.

"It's not a problem with the wiring. Could be the product itself. You'll have to get in touch with the manufacturers."

"Can't you stop it now?" Mavis said, with a tone of desperation she had not intended to use today.

"I'm afraid not, madam."

The repairman straightened up and made towards the door.

"But I don't know who the manufacturers are," Mavis bleated to the repairman's back as she trailed behind.

"It'll be in the documentation that came with the machine."

"But my husband bought it. I wouldn't know about any documentation."

"I'm sorry, love, can't help you."

Mavis watched out the kitchen window as the repairman made off in his van. She expected to see a smug smile creep across his face. But it didn't.

After making herself a cup of strong tea she sat warming her hands to the mug, viewing the microwave blinking 'FUCK OFF' at her in vibrant red letters. There must be something else she could do. It was true she hadn't gone through Harold's detritus. There was enough of it to make her eyes water, so many pieces of paper with such small print, so very many electrical devices and bits of plastic. What had he planned for it all?

Mavis thought about getting their son to help but she was embarrassed she'd let it get this far. The machine had called her a 'CUNT' last week, and even though Brian was now in his forties, and had probably seen a few of those, as his mother she didn't want to expose him to that kind of language.

Besides, Brian had told her she was not to disturb him for any more nonsense. She was only allowed to dial his number if she'd fallen down or some kind of disaster was imminent. She'd asked what categorised as a disaster - it was always a good idea to be clear about these things - but Brian had just said he'd make a list.

And he had, in his scrawny hand. His teachers had always told him to write bigger. She used to think maybe this scrawl was a way of hiding his true thoughts. He'd always had an air of authority about him but it had only got worse since he'd shacked up with Sandra.

Mavis dragged her finger down the list trying to identify the letters to form words. She thought one was definitely 'earthquake' which seemed rather unlikely in Cheltenham. There was perhaps a 'tornado'. It was really rather insulting. 'Flood' one of them said. Well, it wasn't like she lived on a river bank but she felt confident the list was heading in the right direction. Perhaps abusive microwave would be at the bottom, under physically aggressive toaster.

'Tree falls on house': okay, that one made sense, especially given the large sycamore two doors down. If it went over it would probably reach the conservatory. 'Stolen Identity': who would want to be Mavis? 'Suspected breach of security': she wasn't sure if that referred to her or the house. 'Burglary', 'Fire', 'Theft - inc. car', and finally 'Aliens!!!'

The word microwave wasn't on there. Nor was there anything about technical malfunctions or being sworn at by anyone, let alone appliances. Should she ring Brian anyway? No, he said no more calls unless the list had been consulted and the issue had been found on there. "No more pointless calls." He said this even when she'd phoned him last month to wish him a happy birthday.

Now the microwave was blinking 'WHORE', which was a new one. It was a stretch to think of Mavis as a whore per se. She'd never accepted money. But it was true that she'd romped about with a few not so gentle men when she was younger, less since she'd been labelled elderly.

"My husband always loved me," she told the microwave but it didn't seem to care. The word was clear and bright red against the black backdrop of the rectangular screen.

Okay, so she'd gone a few over her five man quota. Wasn't that supposed to be the average? Mavis had overshot. Who was counting?

The microwave.

"You don't know me," Mavis said but the microwave seemed to think it did. 'SLAG' it flashed up.

She didn't want Brian reading that. He might start asking questions. It wasn't that Mavis had a shady past exactly but her father had died young and she hadn't known what to do with all that rage.

She searched through the bureau for something about microwaves. Maybe Harold had hidden a note in there. In the bottom drawer, under the details about his car, she found a booklet on an old kettle – maybe five previous. There was a pamphlet on a soup maker she'd never even seen and a guide to the George Foreman Grill. It took her most of the evening to read through them cover-to-cover. The only hint of malice was when the guide stated, 'If the George Foreman Grill overheats, unplug at the wall. In the extremely unlikely event of it catching fire, ring the emergency services.'

Maybe it would be worth calling in the fire brigade. But there wasn't a fire. Or even a cat up a tree. There was just an abusive, ever more personal, microwave.

When she turned out the lights to go to bed the microwave was blinking 'DADDY'S LITTLE SLUT'.

"It's just a stupid dream," she said out loud. "I'm probably just imaging the whole thing".

But then she remembered the repairman. He'd definitely seen the word 'TWAT' appear. And then after ten minutes of him poking about around the back, 'FRAUD'. She suspected the microwave was also racist because when the cleaning lady had popped in with some groceries the other morning it displayed something extremely unsavoury.

Perhaps Mavis didn't even need a microwave. Brian had told her to use it because she had a tendency of forgetting things and burning out the bottom of saucepans. "The microwave is much better for you, Mum. You just put the stuff in, close the door and turn the dial. Simple."

In the morning the microwave had stepped it up a notch. 'DIE BITCH', it read.

"No," Mavis replied. "Not yet, anyway."

She unplugged the thing at the wall.

"I won't be needing your abuse anymore, thank you."

But 'SADOMASICHIST' still managed to somehow spring up on the screen.

"That's a long word," said Mavis. "Where did you learn that?

Technical Appliance College," and she laughed at what she hoped was a defiant pitch.

At lunchtime Mavis cooked some soup on the hob while the microwave, scrolling, told her to get her affairs in order. She pulled up a chair next to the cooker and sat there checking over the lip of the pan. She was worried about a fire so she took it off too soon and ate lukewarm carrot and coriander soup as the microwave blinked 'HAHA'.

If she let the microwave get away with this, what about the washing machine, the dishwasher, the security lights fixed up to the wall above the conservatory? Were they going to start flashing Morse code messages of disfavour at the neighbours?

She went to the bureau and took out the pack of letter paper Sandra had bought her for Christmas - pink flowers in clusters in the margins. It reeked of Sandra's acidic perfume. Why spritz a gift? With a red pen Mavis wrote YOU ARE NOT VERY NICE and propped it up on the recipe book stand which she moved in front of the microwave.

It exhibited the words 'SO WHAT?'

'So, you could use learning some manners.' Mavis wrote.

'FUCK OFF BITCH' the microwave replied.

'Case in point – you're not to use that kind of language.'

'OFF?'

'No, F U C K or B I T C H.'

'DIE SLAG.'

'Your repertoire is also limited.'

'WHAT?'

'You've used that one before.'

'WHY?'

'I don't know why. I've been asking myself the same question.'

'WHAT?'

'Why have you become so foul mouthed?'

'YOU ARE A CUNT.'

Mavis was bored. This obviously wasn't working. There was a dialogue but not a very progressive one. She put the stationery away and read the Radio Times.

For lunch she wanted beans on toast and she couldn't be bothered with the chair thing again. She plugged in the microwave. With the beans inside she turned the dial and the whirring sound kicked in. The numbers on the screen counted down to 0 and everything was as it should be. She ate the piping hot beans sitting at the kitchen table with the microwave blinking the word 'BOOB'. Slighted, perhaps it was trying out new vocabulary.

Later in the afternoon she noticed it was showing the word 'BUM'. It was an improvement. Mavis went to bed early feeling like some kind of small victory had taken place. She hadn't called Brian. She had taken the matter of the microwave into her own hands and had at least somewhat improved its manners. Enough with this nonsense, she'd taken back her house.

When she went into the kitchen the next morning she headed for the kettle to make some tea. As she waited for the satisfying click, Mavis went cold. The microwave was on, as usual, and against the black background the red words 'OUR LITTLE SECRET' were beaming out at her.

She was still in her slippers and dressing gown but she unplugged the machine and manhandled it off the sideboard. It was a lot heavier than she imagined so she dropped it on the floor to an almighty crash. Grabbing the cable she dragged it along behind her, bringing the rug. She yanked it into the hallway and up over the threshold. The driveway was soaked from a recent downpour so her slippers were sodden by the time she made the curb but Mavis kept on tugging the thing down across the pavement. The microwave was now blinking 'LOVE ME' but Mavis kicked it instead so it rolled over on its back and into the road.

"And you can stay there and rot," said Mavis. "Or whatever you things do."

And then she had a thought. "That's right, roll over and die, bitch."

A couple who were walking their black lab stopped stock-still as she marched back into her house. The space for the microwave gaped so she moved the fruit bowl over. Much more cheery, a happier shade and the bowl clearly didn't feel it necessary to rearrange the grapes into rude shapes or create unseemly noises with the oranges.

Mavis spent the rest of the morning clearing out the bureau. The flowery letter-headed paper followed the five times outdated kettle booklet into the recycling. Midday she heard the lock on the front door and pottered out into the hall to see what the fuss was about. Maybe the cleaning lady had come around with some more food, though Mavis was well-stocked.

It wasn't the cleaning lady. It was Brian.

"Mum, what's going on? Why was the microwave in the road? Ron and Mary phoned me."

Those nosey busybodies next door. Where was their list?

Brian looked fatter. He'd clearly been gorging himself on Sandra's greasy beige cooking. In his arms he was carrying a big black box. Of course it was the abusive microwave. Mavis screamed, "No, put it back!"

It was too late, she'd seen the screen and so had Brian. It was cracked now but the violent red words were clear enough. It read, 'BASTARD CHILD'.

Brian let out a cough which could have meant anything and Mavis, not knowing quite what else to do, found herself with her middle finger in the air.

"Fuck off," she said to Brian. "And take that fucking thing with you!"

Hank's Last Flight

Andrew Westgate

The pallbearers were friends of Hank's. They slipped away from the wake, out through the backyard, and bundled into an old souped-up Chevy, one of Hank's creations, and headed out into the desert.

They stopped where Hank had started his run, touched the scorch marks on the tarmac, stopped again where he had applied the brakes, the molten rubber, where the tyres melted, was still visible. They knelt down reverentially and touched the road where he had left the ground. They whistled through gritted teeth, a ragged, tuneless, litany. This is where Hank must have known he had a bit of a problem, his Chevy Impala was never meant to fly.

They now stood in a semi-circle, at the place where Hank landed, well impacted, on the edge of the crater that was now known as Hank's Hole. It was damned hot, and windy, the rocky terrain, barren and featureless. Looking back down the road they could see the town in the distance, shimmering in the heat haze.

Dressed in black suits, boot-string ties, long hair slicked back, crocodile-skin boots of various colours, it was Hank's favourite attire, heads bowed respectfully, they waited for Billy-Bob, Hank's brother, to start speaking.

"This here's by way of a eulogy." There were a few snickers amongst his small audience, where in hell had Billy-Bob got a word like that? "I know it 'cause I bothered to look it up. Now shut the fuck up and listen. Hank was my older brother, he wasn't the brightest wrench in the toolkit, don't suppose I am neither. He loved Marlene… and little Hank and little Marlene, like those kids were his own, and not mine on account of his infertility. Didn't trouble him none, and it was only the twice… me and Marlene, I mean.

"Hank was a good man. Been tinkering with cars since he was old enough to walk. Stole a few, but he done his time. Yeah, I was proud to call Hank my older brother on account of him being older than me.

"He liked a drink, don't we all. Usually didn't drink when he drove, just before and after. Used to make him madder than hell sometimes, usually after the cops pulled him over and forced him to blow in one of those silly machines they have.

"He was off the road quite a bit on account of the drink driving but that only gave him time to use his imagination. 'What if…' He had a lot of 'what ifs', did Hank, they came to him when he sat on the porch, waiting for Marlene to get back from the Wal-Mart, where she worked as a checkout girl, whoa that uniform used to look pretty and tight on her butt, waiting for her to cook him his dinner. Tortilla's and hot chilli sauce was his favourite.

"See those folks back there at that funeral, they didn't hear none of this 'cause that preacher, he ain't seen Hank in his church since our Momma had Hank baptised, so the preacher don't know shit.

"He don't know Hank's been our friend since first grade, well your friend, I was first grade later, but you know what I mean, we all known him pretty well all our lives.

"Hank wouldn't hurt a fly. He hunted sometimes, coyote mainly, he hated coyotes and prairie dog, and he'd have a go at those wild dogs down near the swimming hole, he was sure they took his fertility when one of them bit him one night. Lucky he was so drunk he didn't realise until he woke up the following morning with only one ball. Hell of a shock, Marlene said he always slept with his hands between his legs after that. Well you would, wouldn't you? Wouldn't want the wife to bite the other one off. Not that I know anything about Marlene and how she pleasured Hank.

"And then there was speed. Well he done a bit of marijuana and a few lines of coke. Jonny Churchill, king of the quarter mile introduced him to that 'cause he could see the way Hank was around dragsters, touchin' 'em, hands in the engines, pestering the guys who could afford to run them beautiful machines. Jonny knew Hank wouldn't last the afternoon of the meet unless he had something to distract him. He was speed crazy. He even super-tuned our grandpappy's old Ford truck one time, y'all must remember that. The old boy had to have a pacemaker fitted after they caught up with him two counties over the state line. Shoulda had a parachute Didn't stop 'til he ran outta gas.

"Hank wasn't a quick learner, not so good at remembering things. Maybe if he hadda been he'd a remembered grandpa and his truck and included a parachute in the last car he built.

"He tuned and tuned that old Chevy until it couldn't go any faster but that wasn't good enough for Hank, no sir, Hank wanted to go faster, Hank had to go faster. It was a dream, a need, a desire, god-damned necessary to go so fast that his teeth would rattle and the skin of his cheeks would wobble like they do on the films. He wanted to feel the G force, Marlene on the other hand just wanted him to find her G spot.

"He loved Marlene, have I said that? Met her at the raceway. She was servicing Jonny in the back of his trailer. The curtains were drawn 'cause Jonny reckoned her looks were starting to go but, she had clean teeth, all her own, and a good figure. Hank burst in with news that he'd got another few horse power out of Jonny's engine. Jonny went for a spin down the track and when he got back, he didn't have a willing groupie no more but he sure as hell had a devoted fan, in Hank.

"Kinda cemented their relationship. Hank became Jonny's mechanic and now and then Jonny would let him sit in the dragster. Every once in a while, when Jonny wasn't around, Hank took that baby with the big fat wheels at the back and those little skinny ones at the front down that track at two hundred forty miles per hour. He used to say it was fast, but not that fast. Reckoned Jonny didn't have the balls to go all the way to the National Finals. And Hank had a cast iron ball, so he knew what he was talking about.

"One day Hank asked Jonny how they could get to beat the others all the way down the line, not to give them any chance. Strap a jet engine to her and put your foot to the floor, its the only way said Jonny, laughing.

"On the porch that night, after dinner, and after he had sorted out Marlene, it was a Saturday, he sat looking at his old Chevy, resting there under the desert moon and said to himself, 'What if...' What if I strapped a jet afterburner to the roof, how fast would I go? Don't know until you do it Hank, he said to himself. He obviously didn't consider putting wings on or includin' a parachute.

"One night, a little while later, he called round my place, said he needed a hand picking something up. We had a few beers and left to pick the something up at one o'clock in the morning, out by the USAF base. We wait in the dark, off the roadway, truck turns up, guy gets out in Air Force blue overalls, swings back the tarp covering this hump backed monster on the back of his rig and says, 'This do?'

"Hank goes bug-eyed. Nods his head and we struggle the thing onto Jonny's flat-bed truck, strap it down and tarp it up. Hank hands the guy the biggest wad of notes I ever seen him with, rubs his hands together and we go back to his place, offload the afterburner into the shed, he gives me a wad of notes, tells me to keep quiet and drops me home.

"He broke out his beaten-up Harley D and started riding it again. Marlene kept on at him to fix the Chevy, he'd told her it was broke, and he said he was tryin' ta fix it, needed a few new parts. He was always in the big barn of a workshop leaning against the side of the house. He told her it was a big job, would take a couple of weeks, what with him helping Jonny and all. She said no more about it, if it was being held up because of Jonny that was okay with her.

"Takes a bit of courage to drive a Chevy Impala at three hundred miles an hour plus. Highway Patrol deny it happened. Said Hank never had that jet engine on the roof and didn't press the old button to ignite it when he got up to speed. Said it couldn't happen. So, if it didn't happen, how come the coffin was so light? They couldn't explain that could they? 'cause there was nothing much left of him, or the Chevy come to that, that's why. And we got six different camcorder views said he did that run and we gonna go public on this here Internet thing just as soon as me and Marlene sort out how to make a web site or load it on YouTube or some such thing.

"When Hank took off about one and a half miles back there I like to think he had a smile on his face. Felt the speed he wanted to feel. He lived his dream on his last flight, can't say fairer than that. Not many of us achieve that in a lifetime," he paused to wipe a tear from his eye, tried to cover it up as if it was a bit of dirt got in there.

They pulled the rings from their cans of beer.

"To Hank's Last Flight," he shouted into the disinterested desert.

"Amen," came the chorus from his fellow mourners, glad of the chance to slake their thirsts. My but it was hot out there.

for better for worse...

Paul Doran

Yesterday was a bad day. I was tired, frustrated, depressed. I'm doing all I can. I think she knew me and it helps but I don't sleep much any more. This morning I'm very tired again and I don't know how long I can keep going.

I can hear her now - she's not calling but she needs something. I get up. It's cold, it's early and it's dark. I don't know what day it is but if the carer comes later then it's either Tuesday or Thursday. I'll know about half-past-eight.

She stirs when I touch her as if nothing's changed - we always responded to each other. But I'm sure she doesn't know me, only perhaps that I'm not a stranger.

Now it's time for the kind of routine I never imagined and it helps me to reflect, 'for better for worse'. I don't mean it to sound wrong but I'm old too and I can't seem to find the energy that I need to care for her as I would love to. I lift her from the bed in her room – she's light, it's easy and she doesn't seem to know she's being moved. Together we've had to learn a lot of new personal routines and there's a kind of intimacy now that I wish we'd been able to share when we could have enjoyed it.

Sometimes she smiles just like I remember she did when we first met - she doesn't talk but when I think I feel her squeeze my hand that's enough.

She still likes tea in the early mornings and I help her to sip from a spoon. We hardly ever spill now and mostly she goes back to sleep until the carer comes or until I gently wake her.

I'm asleep when the carer rings.

Tripping up Chanctonbury Ring

Patricia Graham

High on the hill at Chanctonbury, West Sussex, the balmy star-spangled night surrendered to thrashing heavy metal music, dazzling disco lights and lanterns.

Ollie pushed his way through the writhing dancers to join the rest of his gang. How long it would be before the law turned up to spoil their rave he wondered.

Ginge, looked ugly, white as a sheet and shaking. “Have you done, Dave?” he whinged. “I’m clucking here mate.”

Ollie had no time for Ginge, or most of the others in the group. Except for Mick they were a load of twats. Mick understood him and if they met some like-minded brothers, they were planning to split.

He watched their self-appointed leader Liam snort coke. Ollie was hoping he’d choke on it. Liam had been to university and his parents had loads of money so he thought that made him their superior.

Well, Ollie had news for him. Blagging money from your parents didn’t make you better than your mates. Every user needed cash. There was never enough for food, let alone drugs. The money had to come from somewhere.

Ollie patted his pocket. It had served the old girl right. She shouldn’t have carried all that money in her bag. Old dears distrusted banks, and that made them ripe for picking. Anyway, Mick hadn’t hit her too hard. A few days in hospital, and she’d be right as rain. But as he pictured her bruised and battered face, he felt a pang of guilt. He’d have killed anyone if they’d done that to his Gran.

Ollie watched Ginge slither to the ground. “What a crackhead,” he sniggered. Then his grin changed to a frown as he spotted Liam chatting up the new girl, Shazi. Ollie fancied her. She was fit; wasn’t like the other mingers and dressed good. He’d have some of that later. But for now, he was more interested in getting his share of magic mushrooms.

The music went up several decibels and dancers threw themselves about erratically as though each could hear a different rhythm. Then shouts were heard, and the wail of a siren began to compete with the thundering music.

Lights were quickly extinguished, and everyone ran around like maniacs as they searched for hiding places.

The siren drew closer and someone drove the lorry with the music system down the hill, forcing an approaching police van into the rough.

Ollie tried to rouse Ginge, but couldn't budge him. So, he left him to take his chance along with the others.

Powerful torches flashed, criss-crossing the top of the hill as a squad of police officers swooped on the revellers.

Ollie ducked down behind a bush with Mick. He'd never had so much fun.

The mayhem continued, punctuated by a noise of revving as the police brought their vehicle back to firmer ground. Then it droned away with several passengers aboard - one of them being Ginge.

The only sound now was a dog barking in the distance. Stars glimmered, and the moon beamed, bathing the top of the hill with silvery light. Those who'd evaded capture crept from their hiding places and relit the lanterns.

Liam stopped snogging Shazi for a moment and turned to face the group. "You know this is Midsummer's Eve, don't you?"

Everyone looked blank.

"Well," he said. "There's a legend about Chanctonbury Ring on Midsummer's Eve."

"What, of it?" sniggered Mick.

"If you let me finish, you'll find out." Liam gave Shazi another quick snog before continuing, "If a person walks backwards around the circle seven times in an anti-clockwise direction, the devil is supposed to appear with a bowl of porridge."

There were howls of derision, but Liam ignored them. "And if that person accepts the porridge, their wish is granted. There is a snag, though. As always, the devil requires their souls for payment."

Everyone fell about laughing, but drugged up to the eyeballs as they were, a romp around the hill seemed like fun.

After a great deal of argument they eventually managed to agree on what direction was anti-clockwise, and which tree to use as the marker. Then they staggered backwards, tripping over roots and chunks of rock until they'd come full circle, before stumbling on again.

A few circuits later, Ollie realised he'd lost count. But determined to laugh in the face of the legend, he pressed on as others fell by the wayside. He wondered how many before him had tested the truth of the story.

Beginning what he believed to be the last circuit, he discovered to his glee that he was one of only two still standing. Shazi not being one of them. She was passionately thrashing about in the undergrowth with Liam. Not the class act he'd first thought she was.

Then Shazi was forgotten as he and Mick collided. Laughing hysterically, they stumbled for the last few feet. Ollie swung Mick around the tree then raced to the centre of the ring, and yelled "Seven. We've done it."

Nothing happened. It was a bit of an anti-climax.

"I could have told you it was a load of crap," said Dave.

"What, the..." exclaimed Ollie. Green smoke was beginning to fill the clearing. Liam opened his mouth, but whatever he was about to say was drowned by a tumultuous noise. It sounded like a fanfare of tuneless trumpets.

Under the influence of magic mushrooms, even the most bizarre could seem normal, so they were not surprised when a dark looming figure appeared in the green mist and stood towering over them.

Ollie reckoned, with horns included, it was at least three metres tall. The body was like his to the waist, but the lower extremities were covered with fur, and very definitely male. He eyed the backward bending knees and cloven hooves. No doubt about it, it was a demon.

Seemingly impressed, Mick clapped his hands and shouted, "Blinding," Ducking immediately as the thing turned to glower at him with eyes like burning coals.

"It's better than virtual reality," yelled Ollie. "Dead - good. Thanks for coming, Bro." The demon's smoldering gaze turned toward him. He could feel heat. An acrid smell stung his nostrils, and the green mist shimmered.

"Where's the porridge?" sneered Mick. "You forgot the oats."

Snarling, the diabolical creature produced a bowl in its filthy talons, and pushed a ladle at him heaped with porridge. Mick inspected it through bleary eyes - paused - then shrugged. "Okay - what the hell. I accept."

A purring sound replaced the snarl as the ladle was put to Mick's lips and he licked it clean.

Ollie laughed, "What about me? I want my oats." He looked towards Shazi and his mates to see if they'd been impressed by his joke. A chittering sound made him turn back. The ladle was forced into his mouth, and he spluttered as scalding porridge poured down his throat.

"Sumfin' real weird going down 'ere," muttered Dave. "I've snorted all kinds of gear, but I ain't seen nuffin' like this."

The others were silent.

Having suffered the burning gruel, and not known for his patience, Ollie was on a mission now. He nudged the thigh of the demon. "You gonna grant us our wish?"

The hairy legs of the demon fidgeted like those of a horse at the starting gate. Then the terrible head bent towards him, and from dripping jaws it rasped, "State your request."

"Out of this world!" yelled Ollie. He was really excited. "You can stuff coke. Give me a trip of a lifetime…

'…and I'll have the same, mate," added Mick.

There was a whooshing sound as a spear of light smashed into their midst like a thunderbolt. It exploded into a thousand glittering splinters and began to spiral with strobe like intensity.

"Wicked!" Ollie was well impressed.

From beneath the ground came a thumping beat, and Ollie and Mick's hair stood on end as a column of pulsing light surrounded them.

The rest of the party tried to resist the whirling vortex as it threatened to drag them in as well. They clung to each other as twigs and branches ferociously lashed their faces.

The noise began to reach an unbearable pitch, and just when they thought their eardrums would burst, a sudden rush of air lifted them above the trees.

The sparkling shards shot skywards, and darkness folded in to fill the empty spaces. Screams and groans could be heard echoing around the hill as would be revellers crashed down onto thorny bushes.

The silence that followed was absolute.

Dave, the first to recover, peered nervously into the gloom to make sure the monster had gone then grunted, "That was one - bad – trip ... Oo snuffed the lights?'"

The only sound now was his chattering teeth. Where was everyone? Were they all dead? Panicking now, Dave searched the undergrowth for a lantern and by its meagre light he looked for possible survivors

First to appear were Shazi and Liam. Then one by one other members of the gang crept from their hiding places. But there was no sign of Mick or Ollie.

"Probably gone to sleep it off," said Liam. Shazi clung to him as though her life depended on it.

Everyone agreed they'd never tripped like that before. And at least two swore to give up drugs completely.

The next morning, Ollie and Mick woke up feeling like crap in a barren rocky landscape, under the blistering heat of two suns.

Blue Bell Hill

Nina Tucknott

"So…been out with friends?" Jack turned to look at the girl next to him. She was young, about twenty, with hair hanging limp around her face, having been soaked by the heavy downpour. Her jacket and long skirt clung to a curvaceous body like a second skin.

"Yes. Had a bit of a shindig. Went on longer than expected. Missed the last bus..." Her voice was quiet and soft. She brushed the wet hair away from her face and looked at him with huge brown eyes. "We had a pizza at Marco's and then a drink or two. It was for my hen night, you see," she volunteered.

"Wow!" Jack kept his eyes on the road. The rain was steady but playing tricks with his headlights. He dropped his speed as he was finding it difficult to see the sides of the road. "I guess that means congratulations are in order. When's your big day?"

"Tomorrow. Two o'clock." She was trying to pin her hair up with a couple of hair slides she'd found in her bag.

"I wish you all the best." Jack looked at her again and she smiled back sweetly.

"Oh thanks! How kind. Graham, that's my boyfriend, me and him...we're gonna be real happy!" She settled back in the seat and sighed contentedly.

Jack switched the fan on, hoping it would help to dry her hair a bit.

"Have you known him long then? Your husband-to-be?" He reached for a cigarette and lit it with one hand.

"Nearly two years now. Met him at school."

"What a coincidence, it's the same with me and my wife, Susan. We've been together since we were sixteen. Thirty eight years coming up soon."

"That's great! That's exactly what'll happen to me and Graham." She accepted the cigarette he offered. "Thanks for coming along just then by the way. I would have got totally drenched!" She pointed towards the road and they watched as the downpour increased.

Once again, Jack had to drop his speed. In the distance, the rumbling of thunder could be heard.

"They did forecast this you know."

"I know, I know! Dad will be livid! Not exactly dressed for rain, am I?" She giggled as she looked down at her wet skirt.

"Nope. Still, I'm your knight in shining armour. Without me, you'd be walking up the aisle tomorrow coughing like anybody's business." He signalled for a green van to pull out in front of him. "You might have to invite me to the wedding, you know," he teased.

"But of course. Do come!" She looked at him seriously. "Graham would love to meet you, I'm sure."

"Is it a big wedding?"

"If everyone turns up, we'll be 128...that includes Nan. They're letting her out for the day."

"I'm Jack, by the way."

"Ellie. Pleased to meet you." She giggled.

Ahead of them, brake lights flashed and Jack's grip tightened around the steering wheel. For a while they were quiet as he concentrated on the driving.

"Just another few miles now and then you'll be home."

"That's right. And only another fifteen hours and then I'll be Mrs Phillips. Can't wait!"

"Mrs Ellie Phillips, eh? It's got a nice ring to it." Jack drew long and hard on his cigarette.

"Well it's better than Ellie Pond any day! I'm keeping my initials though." She giggled again. "You ought to come you know. My dress is absolutely gorgeous! Yards and yards of satin and the veil reaches right down to my ankles." She moved her arms animatedly as she spoke. "Mum's got me these lovely satin slippers too."

"You'll be all right for the wedding waltz then. I should have had a pair of them. I was awful!" Jack groaned at the memory. "I kept stepping on Susan's toes... and her mum's… and her aunt's… it was so embarrassing."

Ellie laughed. "Oh, we're not doing a proper waltz, you know. Although…" she pointed towards the radio, "I might get Graham to dance to something smootchy, maybe by them…"

They listened in silence as *A Hard Day's Night* came to an end.

"Yeah…Graham quite likes The Beatles...one of their slow ones will do. Nah! Who am I kiddin'? He hates dancing!"

The rain ceased. Jack switched off the wipers and opened the window a fraction. Soon, cool night air filled the car. "Any bridesmaids?"

"Five, as a matter of fact! There's Anna, Janet, Katy and Siobhan - they're my cousins – and Lottie, of course. She's my little sis."

"Next you're going to tell me its top hats and tails!" Jack teased.

"Oh but it is! Mum wouldn't have it any other way. I can't wait to see dad. He hates suits! He's convinced he'll look like a penguin!"

"Poor soul!"

"Oh... don't you worry about him! He does as he's told. Besides, it'll be great! Our family hasn't had a big wedding for ages!" She sighed happily again, bringing her legs up and hugging her knees tightly.

Jack felt caught up in her excitement, not for the first time wishing that he and Susan had had kids.

"Afterwards, we've got the reception in The Lower Bell you know," Ellie continued. "The whole place just for us. Imagine that!"

"You're a lucky lass, aren't you." Their turn off was just ahead of them and Jack slowed down to negotiate the bend by Blue Bell Hill. "Here we are then, bride-to-be. Almost there…"

Turning to look at her, his smile froze as the car wheels screeched helplessly on the wet lane.

He heard himself scream, felt metal being crushed, saw a windscreen come towards him. And then…darkness, nothing, just oblivion.

Jack's watch registered way past midnight when blue flashing lights lit up the darkness as two police cars arrived on the scene.

He felt totally drained. He knew he should get up. Should walk towards the police cars. But he couldn't. He couldn't get up from the grassy bank. It was as if his brain wasn't quite up to issuing commands.

The mobile phone lay next to him. At least he had rung for help.

His head hurt like hell. Concussion probably. And his right arm felt really weird.

"So…what's happened here then?" The voice belonged to a police officer coming towards him, a black note book at the ready.

"I don't know, officer," Jack confessed. "It…I…" He felt totally confused and very scared too. He was supposed to remember something. Something important. But what?

“Can I see your licence, please.”

Jack fished it out of his wallet. The action made him wince with pain. Perhaps his arm was broken?

“Would you mind?” Another officer had appeared and pushed a contraption under his nose.

“What? I’m not drunk! I’ve been to see a client!” Jack felt indignant but obliged just the same, satisfied to note that the breathalyser registered negative. A third officer who had also arrived by now snorted and looked disappointed.

“Going too fast, perhaps?” The first officer scribbled furiously in his notebook while the others, already bored, returned to their cars.

“I was not! The roads are too slippery to go fast! It’s just, it’s just...Christ!”

Jack shook his head from side to side and looked at the officer helplessly.

“It’s just what?” The remark was slightly sarcastic, bordering on impatient.

Suddenly Jack’s brain kicked into gear again. “Ellie. That’s it! It’s Ellie. She...she’s just...disappeared!” He felt panic well up and look around him. “She must be here somewhere! You’ve got to find her! She’s probably hurt...”

“Are you saying someone was with you in the car?”

“Yes!”

The officer quickly spoke into his radio.

“One minute I was talking to her...” Jack continued. “She’s getting married tomorrow, you see – short dress, no long, satin veil, penguins, her Nan, all that jazz. Four, no five, bridesmaids I think she said.” He was babbling on and on. “The reception’s at the pub...” he pointed towards The Lower Bell in the distance. “And then the next minute, crash, bang.”

“I see. Hold on, please.” The officer moved back and went towards the police car nearest to him.

Jack could hear him speak quietly to the others.

“It’s the truth... honest!” he shouted, feeling all panicky. “Her name’s Ellie. Ellie Pond.” His head was throbbing. He looked at his car, still in the ditch, its bonnet crushed against the bank. There was no one in the passenger seat. “I picked her up just outside Chatham,” he sobbed, fighting back nausea. “She’d missed the last bus...”

The officer eventually returned.

“It’s all arranged, Mr Parcell. We’ve called the garage; a

recovery van will be here soon. Meanwhile we'll take you to Aylesford hospital for a quick check up. Everything's fine."

"What do you mean fine?" Jack nearly choked on his words. "You've got to find Ellie first. You hear!?"

"I'm afraid we won't, Mr Parcell..." the officer sighed.

"What the hell do you mean?"

"Well…it looks very much like you gave a lift to Ellie Pond tonight."

"I know I bloody did! I told you so myself!"

"So sad," the officer continued, "she was killed along this lane years back. 1965 I think it was…Night before her wedding and all. Must be her anniversary again..."

Fulfilling the Dream

Rose Bray

Blest was the day when those two young men, Theo and Earl, stopped by our homestead to ask for a drink of water.

"Come in," said Mary Beth. "You're welcome!" We rarely had folks visit us on account of being miles from town. It was a rare treat for us to have someone to talk to.

We were at our lowest that week, lost hope; we couldn't even build each other up. The hot wind and dust had scorched our few crops; the corn stood like sticks crackling in the never ending wind.

Those nice young fellas talked until evening about the amazing place where they lived with Huang Fu and the followers. Mary Beth lit the kerosene lamp and offered them a bit of our soup.

"Thank you, no. We have to get back," they said. I don't blame them, they had that sleek well-fed look, whereas we looked like skin and bone compared to them.

"Would you like to come to one of our meetings?" they asked. "There's supper beforehand."

"It sounds good," I said, "but we have no means of getting there. Our old pick-up just about makes it to town for our few supplies."

"That's not a problem, we'll pick you up in the Buick," they said.

So we went the following week. My, how we enjoyed the trip! Before the meeting, our bellies were filled with pork and vegetables, followed by pumpkin pie, the best I ever did taste.

After that we went several times – treated like royalty, we were! We learned all about The Celestial Movement. Huang Fu is such an inspiring leader. When he says something, you just want to do it.

After discussing it with the leaders, who, were very helpful, we decided to make a will leaving our land to The Celestial Movement. Well, it wasn't worth much and the house was hardly more than a shack. We weren't really living - just existing. And in all of thirty years of marriage, we'd not been blessed with children; the great sadness in our lives.

Since moving to Celestial Ranch, we've had no worries. Three meals a day. Everything decided for us. We do our share of the work of course. With fifty people living here, there has to be organization.

Tonight was special; we were the guests of honour at the monthly banquet, with wine as well! I'd never tasted the stuff before. We've been given a long white robe to wear made of parachute silk left over from the War. Each robe has wide sleeves edged with gold and loops to hook over our thumbs when the time comes to fly.

Our great leader, Huang Fu, stepped out on the platform dressed in a flowing robe with a gold headress. "This will be your greatest adventure,' he said. "Tonight, you will meet your unborn children."

I had always pictured a boy called Seth, strong of limb and I know Mary Beth imagined a little girl called Abigail May, pretty as a picture.

It's the most perfect evening as we board one of these new-fangled helicopters. The sun is just beginning to sink with those wonderful colours you get in the west. There are four of us, none of us had ever been in a helicopter before apart from the pilot and the leader. The noise is deafening!

I hold Mary Beth's hand as we fly over the wild mountains where no one ever ventures. She's filled out and I see again the young girl I'd married when she was just seventeen. All the years of poverty slip away and a joyousness takes hold of us both. The leader gives us the blessing and says it is time.

We slip the loops over our thumbs and hug each other. Mary Beth steps through the doorway before me and I watch as the sun catches the gold on her sleeves; the silk ruffles with the rush of air. She looks just like an angel floating down.

"I'm coming," I call as I follow her.

The Ring

Janet Rogers

Alex picked up the metal ring from the grass. It had slid down among the knotty brown tufts. It was the ring she had been wearing. He'd noticed it on her finger and he'd thought how smooth and shiny it was on her rough, worn hand.

But though her hand had looked so strong he remembered the fragile feel of her shoulders, the bones which seemed to melt under his touch, the coarse woollen dress that felt like silk and slithered from his grasp as though he was touching nothing but the night air.

He shouldn't have come up here to this ancient settlement, not on Midsummer's Eve. But he'd heard the trudge of boots in the lane and watched his friends snaking their way up the hill, guitars slung over shoulders, sleeping bags tucked under arms, rucksacks of food and drink.

He'd been here with them last year but he'd felt strange and uneasy as though he was trespassing, walking over graves and disturbing an ancient peace. Nothing he could define, just a feeling, a tremble beneath the surface of his skin, a dark shadow in his mind. He wouldn't go again this year; he couldn't.

They tried to lure him, though, as they marched past his house. He was about to get into his car and leave the village, escape from the possibility but they'd called to him, innocuous words, a mere invitation and they'd planted the thought, made it sound so normal, reminded him why they were going, simple harmless fun.

"Come on Alex. The sky's clear and there'll be a spectacular sunrise."

"No, not this year."

"Come on."

"I can't."

"What are you afraid of?"

"Nothing." He lied.

"You know where to find us, straight up to the top, the big oak on the left, the usual spot."

"No I can't make it this year."

"See you later."

He got into his car and drove out of the village but as he travelled along the bypass he looked up at the hill. The day was fading; the edges of the trees looked swollen and blurred. He could see the little spots of light like glow worms, and patches of smoke curling into the night sky. It was the place to be on Midsummer's Eve.

He turned at the next roundabout and headed back. He didn't feel he was quite in control. He drove home, parked the car and walked again to the gate. The threads of darkness were gathering and a whisper of breeze rustled the beech leaves. He saw the bonfires on the hillside more clearly, he heard melodic sounds, soft singing and sweet music. The Sirens were at work.

He thought he would just go to the end of the lane and look but as he reached the open ground he felt a gust of wind in his face and he knew he had to go further, to the top, to feel the rush of air as it licked in from the sea.

He wouldn't stay long but he'd take his rucksack and sleeping bag, just in case. He felt his resolve weakening. The rooks were circling above the sycamores, flapping and squawking, harsh, dark sounds.

He remembered that, even as a child, he'd found it irresistible; this great mound of earth, Hesbury Ring, a hill fort built up in the Iron Age. He loved to run around the top with his dog and then, gasping for breath, stare down to the sea, that flat pool of blue, and pretend he was on top of the world.

The feeling of loftiness still pleased him but it was the feeling under his boots, the substance deep in the soil, that sense of history, of a life before, another age, a bare, raw kind of living, brutal and rough that drew him there and also frightened him. Every year the feeling became more intense. He didn't know why.

The lane from his house to the foot of the ring was easy in the dark He'd wandered along it so often. He knew every bush and stone; the flint wall, the long twist of brambles, the beech wood and the leggy hawthorn trees, almost falling to earth, swayed down by the west wind. And then a chalk footpath across open downland, all the while the dark dome of the mound lay ahead, a black smudge on a grey sky.

When he reached the part where the hill stood like a fortress before him, he stopped at the gate and stared into the gloom. He could see patches of white chalk where the path led upwards. So he started to climb, his boots twisting on the jagged flints. The moon came from behind a cloud and lit his way so he could pick a safer path. He reached the outer rim and started round it on level ground now, looking for the way which would lead him to the top.

He thought he would find it easily but with the full thrust of summer foliage, the trees had changed shape and distorted the pattern of the landscape. To one side was a steep incline and he peered over, picking out the dips and swoops of the downland and the cream patches of sheep at rest, reclining in moonlight on the fold of the hill.

The path was a narrow, tight mouth through dense gorse and knots of bramble which snared him as he walked, nicking and scratching his hands so that when he finally reached the top and put his sore hand to his mouth to soothe it like a cat with his tongue, he tasted only the metallic tang of his own blood. He pulled out a handkerchief and bound his knuckles and turned to survey the scene. Now he had the wind in his face and relished the cool rush on his cheek.

All around were little patches of light, flickering flames, and in the air, the smell of wood burning and the hum of music and a whisper of voices, rising up to the summit to be caught by the wind and whisked away.

It felt familiar now. He made out the shape of the tallest oak, its branches reaching out, long arms flailing in the breeze. He wandered towards it, tripping over tufts of grass and lurching forwards. He followed the light of the fire, crackling and spitting out sparks which fell like a meteor shower rushing through the night sky.

"I knew you'd come."

"I wasn't going to."

"No, but in the end you had to."

"Yes."

They laughed at him. He'd told them last year about his unease. And they had made it worse. They'd told him ghost stories about the old flint mine under the hill and about the body of the young woman found in the mine; about the burial mound and ancient customs; about Midsummer's Eve, a time when the veil between this world and the next was thin, and when powerful forces were abroad.

It was alright for them to laugh but Alex felt things they'd never felt. He'd studied ancient civilisations. He'd sifted through tons of earth and discovered old treasures. And although he knew the difference between historical fact and myth, all rational thought deserted him whenever he came up to Hesbury Ring.

He stepped forward and squatted down by the fire, warming his hands, pushing them forward into the flaming light, removing the handkerchief and surveying the thorn damage. He wasn't cold but the heat of the fire calmed him.

Jo strummed his guitar. Amy produced pasties and pies and James had brought thin glasses on long stems for the wine. Alex took a glass and sipped the cool, white wine and sat back, leaning against his rucksack. He started to relax. Cathy was singing and her clear, sweet voice filled his mind and took away stray thoughts.

Later, much later, after they had eaten and drunk and laughed, they unfurled their sleeping bags and slid inside and chatted and slumbered and waited for the dawn.

When the hillside fell silent and Alex was midway between dreams and wakefulness, he felt a soft swishing on his cheek as though a cat's tail was brushing it. He felt warm and secure and in his drowsy state he took no notice. He heard a low rumble like the sound of distant thunder as his friends slept on, a wine induced leaden sleep, heavy breath on the still night air. Then the swishing ceased and he missed the comfort of it and he opened his eyes, squinting up at the stars.

There in the moonlight was the silhouette of a young woman, leaning over him, her hand close to his cheek.

"Help me," she said. Alex sat up but she seemed frightened by his sudden movement and rose as if to move away, but he took her icy hand and pulled her back.

"Don't go," he said. He saw the tangle of her long hair, her sad eyes and the gash across her forehead from which blood trickled.

"Sit down. Of course I can help you," he said. And she sat down again beside him, shivering in her coarse brown tunic. The fire was still bright and in the firelight he saw blood drip from her wound onto the sleeve of his shirt. He pulled a scarf from his rucksack and gently held it to her head, binding it round.

"Whatever happened?" he asked. But he didn't need to ask. He saw around her neck a tiny white fish carved from bone like the one that had been found near the body of the young woman in the mine shaft. He'd seen it in the local museum.

"I'm not sure but I think something fell and hit me," she whispered. She sighed and Alex could see tears filling her eyes.

He got up. "Here, lie down and rest," he said, wrapping his

sleeping bag round her and zipping her up inside for warmth. He sat close by her and held his hand carefully over the wound to keep the scarf in place. She closed her eyes. He lay back on the damp grass and rested. In the morning he would get her help but for now he would let her sleep. And he slept too, a relaxed, fearless sleep.

He had allowed the past to come into the present and it didn't scare him anymore. It was as though the whole of time had been moulded together and life across the ages was but fleeting shadows on the land.

In the morning she had gone. It didn't surprise him. And his scarf had gone too. His friends grinned when they found him shivering on the grass beside his empty sleeping bag. They didn't believe him when he told them about the young woman. But it didn't matter. He didn't expect them to understand.

The sun rose magnificently over the eastern downland, a pink glow which seemed to set the hills on fire. And the birds in the bushes trilled shrill tunes, loud enough to waken the dead.

In the dawn light, Alex picked up the ring from the grass and lay it in the palm of his hand. It must have fallen from her finger. It was proof that she had been there with him; that her spirit lived on and roamed these hills. And then he remembered the wound on her forehead. He looked at his shirt sleeve and saw the stain of her blood and he knew for certain that he had not been dreaming.

Of Goats and Gigabytes

Phil Williams

Could it speak, what would the rich country village of St Paul's Walden tell the wider world of its achievements? This forgotten tract of leafy homes and real ales pubs, where a single goat may watch the residents lives unimpeded by city smog or urban violence. My friends, I am that goat, brought to this village to graze on gardens and keep company the swans. Atop the garden incline I see into many homes and many lives, and have such tales to tell. None, though, is more chilling than that of the man who first dared to devour a gigabyte.

In one of my favourite haunts, of white wall and cobbled drive, lived Graham Thistle, a young gentleman who dared to dream. Oscillating between handyman jobs and nights at the pub, he brought friends back to the warmly lit living room, the wide window facing me larger and more vivid than any of your television screens. I saw chatter that ranged from the vulgar to the political, though always unworldly, secluded in this Walden. Come the age of the internet, though, Graham Thistle saw a great calling as his friends drew facts from the air and praised a monolith of information that had come to form.

One chill night, in 2009, I sat chewing shoe while Graham Thistle entered his living room raging from the loss of a pub quiz. He lamented the younger crowd, too engrossed in internet to be beaten. He spoke to Charles Frame, his older horse-whispering housemate, with fuming phrase, "They sit coddling keyboards and soaking up the words of websites to such capacity that we can no longer compete!"

Charles Frame agreed, complaining that such websites as the Wikipedia were so full and free that a mouse might muster more wisdom than a genius. This thought flung Graham Thistle into a vocal tirade; one he would never come back from.

"With massed information stored in such small size, there is no competing through world worn knowledge. A child may take the tiniest action to possess the greatest of information!" He feverishly tore open his mobile phone to reveal a slither of plastic, thrusting it skyward, "Such an object holds a gigabyte of data, enough for several hundreds of thousands of pages wrote with science and culture and the meanings of things! If we could only contain these files within ourselves so easy as they are contained within this disk, we might compete with ease!"

"If but were possible, Graham Thistle," said Charles Frame.

I paused my gentle chew of the shoe.

Simple Charles Frame did not see the downcast gaze of his friend, but there past an unmistakable shadow on Graham Thistle's face. The crossing of some dark plan. The result was not immediate, but us goats are a patient beast, and I let hours pass into the night waiting for what I knew would come. My viewing window was dark for a time, but lit up anew, in the unholy witching hour. Graham Thistle rushed into the living room, straight to the computer. He clicked furiously, throwing stolen glances over both shoulders. Then he sat back holding the phone's plastic disk aloft like an Olympic torch. He cackled as he stood, hungrily eyeing that morsel.

Before my very goat eyes, Graham Thistle thrust the gigabyte into his mouth and chewed it savagely, eyes lit up with a madman's success. His jaw moved with goat-like form, vigorously working this way and that, but he had not the patience of a goat, and he strained to swallow, between laughs, thrusting shattered parts of plastic back into his mouth when they slipped out. He did not notice his mouth bleeding, and forgot to turn off the lights when he left the room.

I waited through the next day, to understand what I had seen in that midnight feast. Graham Thistle showed no signs of change in the morning, bar the odd hiccup of delight, and it took the coercing of his girlfriend Harriet to draw some audible explanation from him. She noted the smug look on his face and demanded an answer. He kept the secret for all of ten seconds before taking her aside, holding her by the hands.

"I did it, Harriet! Would you believe any man could do such a thing? A whole gigabyte, crammed with the information of that monster Wikipedia. It's part of me now, I can feel it in my veins."

Enthralled, Harriet asked him to tell her something. He turned away, though, murmuring, barely audible, "No, Harriet. I must rest. To release it now would be too soon."

As Charles Frame had not seen the plan first emerge, so Harriet did not now see that first seed of deception, and the arrogance growing in him. A goat sees these things, though, and I determined to witness their conclusion.

That evening, when Graham Thistle joined Charles and Harriet to watch TV, his friends regarded him with eager looks. Once or twice Charles Frame excitedly asked the answer of a television quiz question, but Graham Thistle responded with a variety of excuses. First, he insisted he did not want to ruin it for them, then he claimed tiredness. Finally, he snapped, to silence Charles Frame, "Why should I answer your questions, how will you learn if not by yourself?"

Moments of hurt silence passed before Harriet took pity on poor Charles Frame and calmly asked, "Could you not share just one answer? It would please us so."

"Very well," huffed Graham Thistle, and he awaited the next quiz question.

The choices were evidently displayed for him on the screen, and the moment he read them he confidently blurted out the answer, "A monomer."

The hope in the faces of Harriet and Charles Frame turned to confusion and disappointment. He was wrong. Slight panic crossed Graham Thistle's expression, and he stuttered, "I - I do not know all. It has not entered my blood entirely. And I only have a gigabyte, when there is close to five out there."

They let this pass.

He was still a hero, after all, and behind that panic was a determination to do more.

As evening set in, I ignored the farmer's call, to not miss a beat of the experiment taking place. I could see in the shadows of the upstairs bedroom that all was not well. After arguing in silhouette against the curtains, Graham Thistle abandoned Harriet to return to the living room. I shared in his isolated worry as he sat holding his face. Sorrow ran from the cuts in his mouth and the shame that quiz had laid on him. He looked my way and our eyes met. In that instant, the next stage of his plan grasped him. A wicked grin spread across his face as he shared the secret with me. He scrambled to a drawer, turned his computer on, and began repeating what I had witnessed before. He put more information onto disks, found more of the small objects amongst the cluttered living room, and devoured them all. No devilish possession has better captivated me than the private theatre of that young man crunching plastic and loudly laughing. Blood crept from his lips, and his enthusiastic saliva sprayed sordid blots of red across the furniture and carpet.

He crashed against the window pane, palms facing me as he stared out. Still chewing. Bits of bloody metal and plastic trickled out as he messily laughed, sharing the joke of his glory with me alone.

What a scene for Harriet to walk in on.

His face fell when my flitting eyes betrayed her entrance. He turned, still chomping, and she screamed. She ran, but he caught up to her, overpowered her and pinned her to the floor. As she struggled he spluttered into her face, "Don't you see? I have it all, now! Four and a half gigabytes, all inside me! Wikipedia is forged into my soul, there is nothing I do not know!"

"You're mad!" she shrieked, "It's too much! No man can digest that much!"

She beat her fists against him and he released her, sitting back on the floor. She jumped up to flee but paused in the doorway when he didn't follow. She shook her head and said, "I never judged you for your intelligence…until now."

He was not angry. He laughed and cursed her ignorance, said he no longer needed her. Harriet left as Charles Frame came in. He stared in horror at the sight of his friend. Graham gargled blood in his direction, then strode past him. Away.

Charles said nothing.

When the curtains opened in the morning, Graham Thistle was still encrusted with gore and unchanged from his evening clothes. He slumped into an armchair, exhausted. Charles Frame cared over him, bringing him tea. Graham took his housemate's hand and said, "Do not worry for me. I know of the world, now. It all makes sense."

"Tell me," Charles Frame pleaded. "Tell me of what you know, please."

"I cannot," Graham Thistle said. "For I have too great a burden to bear. Great knowledge requires great management, Charles. Give me time."

Charles Frame left him with a sad look of admiration, off to start the day's work.

Graham Thistle reclined deep into his seat and went nowhere. The sun bathed the living room in warmth and light, but the house was dark in soul. Shortly after Charles Frame left, Graham retched forwards, raising a fist to his mouth and coughing uncontrollably. Fresh blood mixed with the congealed mess already dried about his lips.

As the day progressed, he got worse. The coughs started gradually, occasionally interrupting his patient sitting with small eruptions of blood and looks of great pain. Then came the groaning. He clutched his hair and rolled his eyes, letting out the base howl of an injured beast. Then came the tumbling, as he dropped to his knees and attempted to crawl away. He spasmed into a coughing fit and fell onto his back, moaning. The next coughs sent blood up like a fountain, falling into his nostrils and his eyes. He clawed at himself screaming "Get it out, get it out!"

With a last burst of energy, Graham Thistle lunged at the window, meeting my eyes again, and his hands smeared red down the pane as he dropped once more to his knees. He told me, weakly, "It was too much. Too much for any one man."

He twitched and coughed and occasionally sobbed, in turn holding his head and his stomach. It went on for painful hours, this man's maddening decline, but after the lunge at the window he showed no further capacity for speech and no ability to move more than the tremulations of his enfeebled limbs. With one last cough, with no one else to see it, his new knowledge pushed life itself out of Graham Thistle's eyes. His head rested in the blood that the gigabytes had forced out of him.

I paid private vigil to Graham Thistle.

This was the folly of the 21st Century Man, found here in the reclusive St Paul's Walden: the need to keep pace with advances proved ultimately self-destructive. This, I felt, is what the small village would say to humanity, if it had a voice.

When Charles Frame returned he let out bawling fits of screeches, clutching at dead Graham Thistle's chest and asking why of the world. There was no answer for Charles Frame, except that one thing was to blame. He threw pointing fingers at the computer in the corner, damning Wikipedia and all who used it, damning gigabytes and terabytes and all that come with them. In vengeful fury he tore wires and chips from that computer and ran out of the house with fistfuls of broken technology. He hurled them over the fence, towards me, with a strangled cry "You have hurt your last heart here, Wikipedia!"

As the debris rained around me, I considered carefully dear Graham Thistle, and what he had really achieved. Bearing such truths in mind, I continued to chew the shoe.

God Bless Gary

Cherrie Taylor

"Sit down," she said. "I've got something to tell you. Something you're not going to like."

I was on my way out, but the look on her face stopped me cold. "What is it?" I asked, wishing the words didn't taste of fear.

"Sit down!"

I looked around - the only place was the floor or the toilet. I flushed it out of habit and sat down. She towered over me with the brush in her hand like a weapon.

"For Christ's sake Harriet - tell me what's up?"

"He's down there," she said, pointing the brush at the U-bend.

"You said you'd wait – see if the cough improved."

"Improved! It's been 100 days - just how long should I have waited - for the moon to turn to cheese?"

I could tell she was mad and how could I blame her. "Harriet love, let's move out of here to somewhere more comfortable." The toilet brush was becoming more than its parts as she brushed it in my beard.

"It's easy for you. You've not had to listen to the constant hacking. It was the kindest thing. The papers from Dignitas are down there too. Your flush will have eased the blockage."

I stood up and lifted the lid. I've always had a fear of the toilet monster. I held my breath and looked down. The use of Harpic original seemed to have eliminated 100% limescale, 99.9% bacteria, viruses and stains and Gary. God bless him.

The Feathering of Peacocks

Audrey Lee

A woman once stayed in her house, waiting for God to hear her prayer. She did not pray with words, for she had carried in her chest a weight so heavy with entreaty for so long that words were unnecessary. She craved his favour not for herself, but for her son, who had recovered from a wasting disease and was now growing frighteningly fat.

She waited for three days - maybe three whole weeks or months - who knows; she was not sure herself. While she waited her son grew so fat that he could not squeeze into the largest of his trousers. She spent many hours cutting and sewing cloth to cover his bulk.

Her son grew fat seemingly without reason, for the dinners she gave him were calculated calorie by calorie. The great feasts she had made to tempt him from starvation: turkey dripping and potatoes, bread and butter puddings, stilton cheese and walnuts, fried bread and marmalade and other delectable combinations were a thing of the past. Now, she kept the larder under lock and key.

On the third day, or maybe week or year of her wait, the woman sat in her usual position – upright, facing the window, hands folded in her lap. Her body was so leaden that she could hardly bear the weight of it.

First she heard a shuffling on the stairs, and after a pause a rasping of overworked lungs, and then a shape she barely recognised lumbered into the door-frame and pulled and pushed its way through.

"Mother," cried a tiny mouth from within deep folds of flesh, "I cannot bear this life you have given me."

When the woman saw that nothing she had done had helped her son one jot, neither the lock on the larder door, nor the tailored trousers, nor the good advice she had bestowed on him in his distress, she became exceedingly angry with God and ceased expecting him to hear her. She decided that she must take desperate measures of her own. She would leave her son and go on a very difficult journey to visit a herbalist she had heard of who could concoct magic potions, but could she carry for so long a distance the weight inside her chest, which had now become as heavy as a cooking pot? She stood up to test her strength. Yes, her body held together. She must go. It was then that she noticed a small but beautiful bubble floating on the air before her. The bubble was intangible as bubbles are; when she put out her hand to touch it, it dissolved and unexpectedly reformed itself.

"Mother, do not leave me!" cried her son, when he saw that she was preparing for a journey, but the woman steeled herself and with many kisses and embraces explained that for his sake she must go.

Through many streets and villages the woman walked heavily, weighed down by her body. She looked at the people she passed, busily shopping for vegetables or talking to each other, and wondered whether they, too, were attempting to guess in pounds and ounces the weight inside their breasts; she thought not. She saw that these people smiled and laughed, spoke in bantering voices and moved with light skipping steps; some carried no weight at all, she reflected. Hers had assumed the density of a lead ball. A surgeon could dissect it with a knife, she thought, and there it would be, black beneath the ribs, all bloodied in the gore of lights and lungs and twice as real as any vital organ. When she thought this, she fell to the ground and wept bitterly all through the first night of her journey. In the morning she discovered that her tears had lightened the weight, and when she had dressed and breakfasted, and set out on her journey again, she was comforted to observe that the bubble had reappeared, and floated gently before her.

When, many weeks, months, or maybe years later, the herbalist saw the woman approaching, he was standing at the upper window of his house collecting the dried senna pods that lay along the window sill. He was wondering how many pea-pods could be mixed with them before his clients noticed (senna pods were so expensive). The woman must be very rich, he decided, for although she looked exhausted and bedraggled, she had managed to acquire the most exclusive of accessories, a large and luminous bubble that floated just above her head.

The woman could not believe the trouble that the charming herbalist was prepared to go to for her sake. He listened with the utmost concern to her problem, and was prepared, he said, to spend many hours, days, weeks if necessary, pouring over his books for exactly the right remedy. Indeed, the woman spent several days and nights in the shop while bottles of every size and shape, pills of every hue, special techniques of massage and diet and exercise, perfumes and aromatic oils, were piled on the counter. The woman was confused – which to purchase? Naturally enough it turned out to be the tiniest but most expensive of all the concoctions. She was to give a drop three times a day with absolutely no food. A hot rush of anxiety momentarily assailed her, but the savings she had stowed inside her bodice were still there, and just enough. Dear lady, she was told, did she not realise that this certain and assured remedy for fatness would earn her the undying gratitude of her son?

Outside the shop it occurred to the woman that she now had to travel home without money for food or shelter. The thought of her son, who by now must have been the size of a whale, spurred her on and by begging she managed to survive. When at last she returned, exhausted and fearful, she stood trembling on the steps of her house for several hours, days, or was it years, before she could push open the door to face whatever sight would greet her.

But what is this? At her table sits a young maiden with rosy cheeks and smiling lips. On her table is a healthy meal of bread and cheese, fruit and salad. There are signs that many healthy meals have been provided over many days: baskets of apples and vegetables, plates that have been washed and dried and put away. There is tea in the old china pot and two cups and saucers. The young girl is gazing into the eyes of her son and he, a perfectly acceptable shape, is holding her hand. There is murmuring and smiling of secrets, and glimpsing of rainbows through the windows. Their talking is an exploration into virgin territory, a trail blazed through a jungle, an unexpected rain on iron ground, a wonder like the feathering of peacocks. The larder and the lock are sloughed off like a ship's bottom of barnacles, forgotten as the blubber and the toothpick limbs, forgotten as the mother...

Who is this maiden? It does not matter who. She is the young man's destiny.

The woman gasped with joy and threw the herbalist's remedy into the unfathomable heaven. Truly, she thought, I see that all the time God had heard my prayer. Now, lightness bore her irrepressibly upward, and she sprang into the air and danced above the common ground. No skylark sang that day more joyfully, no drowning person saved from death with more gratitude. When her son heard the sound he, too, laughed for sheer happiness.

Very soon the woman, knowing that there is a time for all things, cheerfully bade her son goodbye as he left her house to make a home of his own. The bubble, which had never really left her, was then at its most beautiful and luminous.

The Here and Now

Pat Hopper

I have never been worried about the *hereafter* - I've been too busy living. But, eyeing the naked body of the beautiful blonde, I knew that this was the *here and now*! My hair trying to stand on end, I backed away from the bed. The body sprawled on the duvet, a gun tucked in one hand, was mine.

Just to be sure, I glanced in the mirror on the wardrobe door. No reflection, at least not of me. I looked back at the gun. It shouldn't have been there. It wasn't mine - I wouldn't touch one with a bargepole: they're lethal. And this one had given me a hole in the head, which probably explained my confusion.

My memory being hazy, and with too many gaps, I wondered how long I had been hanging around. The window was letting in daylight. But why was it open? Going by the way the curtains were flapping, it was also letting in an icy blast. So much for central heating - I was glad I couldn't feel the chill.

Groping for an answer, I bridged a gap. Jet lag! I had been on holiday in Tenerife and had flown home last night. My suitcase was half unpacked, my clothes scattered around and my nightie on the floor. It should have been on my body. Staggering to bed, I must have pushed the window open forgetting that I was back in mid-winter London.

But I hadn't forgotten what to do next. Being only too obviously dead, I waited for a tunnel to appear. I like ghost stories so I knew what to expect. I would enter the tunnel, head for the light and all would be well.

When nothing happened, I was suddenly aware that if I hadn't killed myself - and I was sure that I hadn't - someone had done it for me. I was alone in the room, the door was shut; but my killer could still be in the flat - unless they had left by way of the window which didn't seem likely. The house didn't have a fire escape and my flat was on the fourth floor. It was a long way down to the ground.

I went to the door and threw myself against it. It was like hitting a brick wall. It didn't hurt, but I rebounded. So much for the newly dead rising from the grave; they wouldn't have got past the coffin lid. As for blood-curdling screams, all I could produce was a whimper.

But, as well as ghost stories, I like murder mysteries, though I wasn't that keen on being the victim. Carefully avoiding my body, I sat on the bed. I had been murdered and there had to have been a motive. According to the authors the usual motives were hate, revenge or money. Or something on those lines. But revenge was out; as far as I knew nobody hated me. And I didn't have any money: I'd spent most of it on the holiday.

I looked at the dressing-table. If I'd still had a heart, it would have sunk. The motive wasn't money, but it had been theft. I had left a large sealed envelope propped against the mirror. It was gone. I must have disturbed the thief while he or she was stealing it and, being a witness, I had been killed.

In the envelope was a book that didn't belong to me, which made it worse.

Before becoming a *dear departed*, I had been a hairdresser working in a salon where my landlady was the cleaner. She was the widow of an army officer who had spent most of his money backing knock-kneed horses and, as a result, she was often strapped for cash. So when I was looking for a flat she had let me have hers - at a reasonable rent - and she had moved into the adjoining one, which was cheaper.

She had also introduced me to her nephew, Jason. It was so romantic. As soon as we met, we had fallen in love. Jason would have come to Tenerife with me if his boss, a turf accountant, hadn't been too mean to let him have the time off. It was a package holiday and, as I'm very fond of my landlady, I was pleased when she offered to accompany me in his place.

It was in Tenerife that the envelope had come into my possession – quite by mistake. The manager of our hotel had found the book at a local market and wanted to get it valued in London. Since he didn't trust the post he had asked my landlady if she would take it back with her. She is an obliging person so I wasn't surprised when she said that she would. He was very grateful and told her that someone would come and collect it from her. But, while we were packing, it had ended up in my hand-luggage where I didn't discover it until we were home. She had already gone to bed so I hadn't disturbed her.

But whoever was supposed to collect the envelope must have been in a hurry and got the wrong address. They had come into my flat instead of hers.

Hearing a sound coming from the hall, I thought it was the murderer. But they must have left my front door open. It was Jason who walked in.

Spotting what awaited him, he stared aghast at the gun.

"Jessica, darling," he groaned, snatching his mobile out of his pocket. "What have you done?"

"What have I done?" I was standing right behind Jason. He didn't hear me but he must have sensed my presence. Mobile at his ear, he shivered and looked over his shoulder. If I had been able to shed tears, I would have shed them as he took a quick, shuddering breath then shouted at whoever had just answered his call, "Ambulance, quick - my girlfriend's shot herself."

"It was murder," I said indignantly. He shivered again - sensing me was all he could do.

But I still didn't know how long I had been dead and, much as I loved Jason, I didn't want him joining me, which he could have done if the murderer was still in the flat. The bedroom door now open, I headed for it, dodging round him in case I was as unsuccessful at walking through people as I was at walking through walls. I didn't want to scare him.

I ran down the hall. I didn't try *wafting* but stuck to the tried and tested, one foot in front of the other. The lounge, kitchen, and bathroom doors were open, but if anyone was in there, they were out of sight. The wailing of sirens heralding the arrival of the ambulance, I rushed back to the bedroom and glanced out of the window. A police car had arrived as well.

I wondered, briefly, if suicide with a gun was always classed as a suspicious death. Good for you, I thought as a WPC and her partner, a burly PC with a clipboard, came in to survey my mortal remains. They were followed by the paramedics with a stretcher.

"Over there," said Jason pointing to the bed.

To my dismay, the gun being close to my head, the hole showing powder burns and apparently my fingers smelling a bit iffy, the officers decided suicide was the correct diagnosis – once they had been told where I was supposed to have got the gun.

"It's my husband's old service revolver," quavered a voice coming from behind the paramedics. "I shouldn't have told dear Jessica where I'd hidden it."

My landlady was the murderer? She was lying through her yellowing teeth; she had never even told me she had a gun.

"Why did you hang on to it, Aunty?" cried Jason, keeping his eyes averted as the paramedics slid my body onto the stretcher,

"I didn't want to part with it." The tear, dribbling down her wrinkled cheek, satisfied the officers. The WPC gently warned her that she wouldn't be getting it back then, after taking Jason's name and address, asked him when he had last seen me.

Poor Jason. He looked sick as a parrot. I wanted to kiss him, but decided in time to keep my lips to myself.

"Last night," he said, his voice unsteady. "She'd been away so I called in to welcome her home. I should have stayed with her." My mortal remains departing out of the door, he cleared his throat with a painful rasp. "But I could see she wasn't herself."

"It was jet lag," I shouted, wasting my non-existent breath.

"Was she prone to bouts of depression?" asked the burly PC.

"I wouldn't have said so: she was always so bubbly." Having confirmed my opinion of myself, Jason shook his head slowly. "When she opened the window and threatened to throw herself out, she was laughing. I thought she was joking."

I could scarcely believe what I was hearing. Of course, I would have been joking. Jet lag or no jet lag, I would never have been that stupid: I don't like heights unless I'm safely in a plane. Thinking about it, I hoped the *hereafter* didn't include flying.

Jason slumped on the bed. "If only I'd realised…"

"It's not your fault," said my landlady, patting him on the cheek.

"Of course it is, Aunty," he whispered.

After the officers left, he went to the window and looked down. He was so upset he didn't sense my presence as I peered over his shoulder to see stretcher and paramedics enter the ambulance.

My landlady came and stood at his side. She chuckled. "You saying goodbye to the nosey little madam? It's her own fault; she shouldn't have opened the envelope."

I let out a whimper that she didn't hear – she had filled in the final gap.

When I'd discovered the envelope, I had yielded to temptation. It was self-sealing, but with a little help the flap had lifted. The book being so old I couldn't read the title on the cover, I had peeked inside. The pages had been replaced with a cellophane bag of what looked like talcum powder. I've seen enough thrillers to know what it was! What I had carried through Customs had been a consignment of drugs. I was so shocked, I'd opened the window. But I hadn't had time to close it. As I emptied out the contents, Jason had rushed into the room.

He wanted the book and my landlady had given him the gun in case my memory needed jogging as to where it was.

So I had given it to him, told him what had been in it then pointed to the window. He hadn't been happy. Losing his temper, he had shot me. It had happened so fast, I hadn't even had time to whimper.

But I made up for it now, and this time Jason heard my voice. And so did my landlady. My blood-curdling scream shocked them off-balance and, grabbing each other, they left by way of the window.

It's a long way down to the ground.

My Name is Tony

Ian C. Black

Finding the back door open, Tony went outside. He liked being outside; inside was hot and stuffy, but here the garden was warm and sunny and wide open. He could hear the birds singing and all sorts of other interesting noises. It was the churning and clunking from the side of the house that made him go to investigate. But all was quiet when he got there, except the gate swinging on its hinges.

"The gate's normally shut," he thought and, taking the opportunity to explore, went through into the front garden. He could hear the churning noise again, but quieter than before. He ventured outside the front gate, and further up the road he saw a large lorry, with men emptying wheelie bins on hooks into the back of it. The nearer he got to the lorry the worse the smell. He didn't like it anymore.

Tony realised he was outside, he never went out on his own.

"Why not?" he thought. "I could just go to the park." Tony set off down the road. He'd been there many times before and knew the way. There were no busy roads to cross, so he was quite safe. When he got to the park it was wide and open. He walked across the grass and up into the trees where he had often hidden from his mum. She'd shout at him to come out, but he'd stay there until she clambered in to fetch him and they'd both laugh.

As he came out of the other side of the trees, there in front of him was the playground. It was empty, inviting, almost calling to him. Tony wandered inside and had a go on the swings, but they seemed too close to the ground. Then he had a few goes on the slide. That was fun, but it seemed to be a smaller one now; not as tall as he remembered. Next was the roundabout. Tony set it turning and jumped on. He almost fell off again, but managed to hold on long enough to get his balance. He was having great fun.

Suddenly his enjoyment was interrupted by someone shouting. Tony immediately looked towards the old building where the park keeper stayed. Would he be told off? There was no one there. Then he saw them. A group of big boys; bullies. Tony was quite frightened of the big boys, but didn't want to show it. He let the roundabout slow down and then walked back to the swings, as they were furthest away from the big boys. He was just sitting on one when a stick landed next to him. He looked over at the big boys, two of them were fighting and they were all getting much closer to him. Tony was really scared now. He got off and tried to run away from the big boys. He fell over. It hurt, but he wouldn't cry. The big boys stopped fighting and looked at him, he didn't want them to get any closer; and they were laughing at him. Tony clambered to him feet and ran as quickly as he could out of the playground and the park.

He was over the wrong side of the park now and the road was unfamiliar to him. He could find his way home through the park, but not with the big boys in there. So Tony started to walk along the path by the road. It was a busy road and quite fun to see all the cars and lorries racing passed. It didn't matter where he was going it was an adventure.

Tony continued to walk the now darkening streets; he had no idea where he was or where he was going. The fact it was dark told him it was late, apart from this he wasn't good with time. He knew he was getting hungry as he continued to trudge along. He'd thought he could find his favourite shop and get some sweets; but he hadn't been able to. He didn't know where he was.

"Should I go back?" he thought. "Perhaps it's this way, or maybe that?" Tony knew he shouldn't talk to strangers, so he didn't ask anyone where he was or how to get home. Not that he knew where home was anyway. Now it was dark, he was becoming frightened. He hadn't been out in the dark, alone for - well he couldn't remember - he was confused. The lights all around him made everything look so different. The cars were scary at night, so he walked close to the fences and walls, to keep as far from the road as he could. That's when it happened! Walking too close to a fence, he didn't see the wood sticking out at the bottom in the shadows; he tripped and fell.

Tony opened his eyes and was blinded by the bright lights. His head, his legs, his arm, they all hurt. He wasn't really sure why; but he knew they hurt. Where was he? He was lying on a hard bed, quite high off the ground and there was a strong smell of cleanness. A woman in a nurse's uniform came up to him.

"Hello, what's your name?" she asked. Tony lay there unsure what to do, so he said nothing. He couldn't remember his name anyway.

"I'm Jenny, you are in hospital, but there's nothing to worry about, you've had a little accident. You'll be fine. I just need to let someone know you're here, so can you tell me your name?"

"I... I don't know." Tony replied. He thought he should say something to her as she was being so nice to him. But what could he tell her.

"How about a drink of water?" she said, sitting him up a little and pouring the water into his mouth. Tony didn't have much choice really, so he drank some.

"How I hate water," he thought to himself as he swallowed. After this the nurse chatted at him as she took his clothes off and got him into a white coat, which she put on backwards; even Tony knew coats do up at the front. Then a man in a white coat - the right way round, so obviously not dressed by Jenny - came over to see him.

"Hello, I'm Peter. What have you been up to?" he asked.

"I don't know," Tony replied, to the man who had such a friendly face, filled with a really big smile.

"Well, you seem to have been in the wars a bit. But we'll soon have you fixed up and trotting off home."

"Do you know where I live?" Tony asked.

"I'm sure we'll find that out very soon," Peter replied, looking across at Jenny.

"Don't you worry about anything," said Jenny. "Just lie still and we'll sort everything out." As she said this, Tony could see someone else in a uniform behind her. But this was a dark uniform, not someone there to help. It was the police.

"What have I done," thought Tony, he knew who the police were and that it wasn't good if they were there to see him. Slowly the policeman approached. He smiled at Tony, Jenny and Peter.

"This policeman has come to find out where you live," said Jenny.

"But I don't know."

"We know that," said the policeman, "that's why I'm here."

Tony was very confused at this. Why come and see him to find out something he didn't know.

"Can I have a look at his clothes?" the policeman asked Jenny. She produced a bag from behind Tony and handed it to him.

"We found this," she said, producing a piece of paper. It wasn't something Tony remembered being in his pocket. "We rang the number, but there was no answer."

"We'll sort this in no time," said the policeman. He smiled at Tony to reassure him. Just then, Tony heard another voice. The policeman turned to his radio and spoke into it. He read the information from the piece of paper and waited for a reply. This caught Tony's interest. He'd seen things like this on TV. This was exciting now, much more fun than walking around, even the playground.

After a few minutes, the other voice was back. The policeman spoke a couple of words in reply and turned to Jenny.

"They've been out looking for him; they're on their way here now. About 30 minutes I'd say; and his name is Tony."

"Great," said Jenny, and she turned to Tony. "You'll soon be off home, Tony."

"Yes! Tony, that's my name," he said and smiled at Jenny. After that he was left alone. The policeman left, Jenny and Peter went to talk to some other people, he could see them walking around. Occasionally Jenny would come over to him and smile.

"Are you okay, Tony?" she would ask, but not really wait for a reply as she hurried past.

All of a sudden there was a lot of noise, Tony became quite unsure and wanted to leave. He tried to get off the bed, but it was quite high. Jenny caught him as he was trying to get down.

"Where are you going," she said, quite abruptly.

"I need the toilet," said Tony, the first thing that came into his head.

"You'll have to wait a minute. It's very busy at the moment. I'll be back as soon as I can. Okay?" She put him back on the bed and rushed off again. It was only a couple of minutes later when some different uniformed people came rushing in with someone on a bed on wheels. They pushed her past Tony and he could see she was covered in blood. This frightened Tony.

"What had she done?" he thought. "Had they done something to her because she didn't do what she was told?" Some more people in the same uniforms pushed a man in. He had blood on him and something wrapped around one leg. He moaned as he went past. Tony really did want the toilet now, but he daren't move.

Tony lay there trying not to think about it, but he was bursting. People kept rushing in and out of the room where the people covered in blood had gone. If he tried to move they would see him, what would they do to him then? Tony was desperate for the toilet, but too scared to move. Then it was too late, he could feel the top of his legs and his bottom getting warm as the pressure released. He couldn't stop it and he began to cry, he knew he shouldn't do this. He wasn't a baby.

As Jenny rushed by she saw Tony crying and stopped.

"What's wrong Tony?" He didn't reply, just lay still and frightened. Lifting the blanket Jenny could see the wet patches on the bed and Tony's clean white coat.

"Sorry," he said, and started crying again.

"Don't worry," said Jenny. "We'll soon have you sorted and ready to go home."

It didn't take long to get Tony cleaned up. Jenny helped him get dressed into his own clothes again and sat him on a chair next to the bed. All this time he had been surrounded by curtains and couldn't see what was happening outside. As Jenny pulled back the curtains, Tony could see a woman rushing towards him. He thought he recognised her; she looked quite like his mother.

"She has found me, come to take me home," he thought, "She'll know where it is." As she got closer Tony could see she was crying, why was she so upset to see him?

"Dad! We were so worried," she said, "We've been looking for you all night. I'm so pleased you're alright." She threw her arms around Tony. "You mustn't go off like that; it's not safe for you."

At last Tony could relax, he was safe again. She would take him home, somewhere he recognised. Home.

"But," he thought, "Why is my mother calling me Dad?"

The Old Canal

Alison Batcock

Stephen sat in the stairwell outside his home, his back against the damp concrete, listening to the sound of his parents' argument echoing off the walls. The words seemed to tumble over each other, like the recent storm he had seen on the news when the waves had thundered on to the shore, crashing on the rocks, one on top of another. But Stephen had never been to the seaside to see it for himself. He much preferred calm, still water like the ancient canal that ran along behind the Manchester tenement block where he lived.

Shivering, he picked up his long-outgrown jacket and hurried down the stairs. 'The sunlight scorched his eyes and he blinked several times. From the bottom of the stairs he could see half a dozen other boys playing football in the yard between the blocks. Most of them were dressed in Man U shirts and Converse trainers. He looked down at his faded t-shirt and stained plimsolls and turned the other way, to weave his way behind the dustbins and over the rusted chain-link fence towards the canal.

He ran along the towpath, kicking empty lager cans into the bushes, and flung himself down on the tarmac path under the railway bridge with a sigh of relief. A bundle of old rags in the far corner unrolled itself to reveal an old man with shaggy white hair and straggly beard. He raised a grubby hand, more like a bear's paw, to Stephen and shuffled closer. Despite the stench Stephen did not move away. The stagnant water gave off its own pungent smell, so there was no point. Anyway, old Roger was Stephen's friend.

Some days they sat for hours just contemplating the changing colours that swirled and re-formed in the sunshine on the oily surface of the water. Other times Stephen would delve into the water with a stick to see what flotsam and jetsam he could salvage. Often Old Roger had a can of cola or lemonade for him. Stephen never asked where they came from, assuming they were probably stolen. Occasionally, Stephen managed to bring some biscuits or a couple of slices of toast from home to share, to show that the kindness was not just one-sided.

"Hello, lad. How's things?"

"Arguing. Again."

Old Roger nodded. It was a familiar story and needed no further explanation or comment.

"Mum's got a new job. But it's longer hours and he doesn't like that."

"More money though. He'll like that?" Old Roger handed Stephen a can.

Stephen pulled back the ring, which he discarded into the water, and took a slug of the drink. "Going to be paid direct to the bank, so he can't get his hands on it." He paused. '"What is it you always say? Mustn't count my chickens…."

"Got to be good news though, lad."

"Mum says that she's going to build up a nest-egg, so that one day..."

They smiled at each other and chinked cans.

"Here's to the future," Old Roger saluted him.

They sat back to watch the sun glinting off the murky water.

The Elastic Heart

Alison Hawes

It must have been about eighteen months after Mum died, that Sue next door turned up at our door one Friday evening.

"Hi. Sorry if I'm late!" she said as she breezed past dad and plonked herself on the sofa next to me. Dad blinked at her short skirt and her nose stud and said, "Were we expecting you?"

"Are you still here?" she giggled, "Come on! Get your coat on and down that pub before they run out of beer. Katie and I are going to have a girls' night in, aren't we?"

"Yeah. Girls' night in! Girls' night in!" I began to chant.

"But.." Dad began.

"Now don't disappoint me, John. Look I've come prepared!" Sue said and pulled a DVD and a large bar of chocolate out of her bag.

"Well, I hope that film is suitable," blustered Dad.

"Look, it's a PG," Sue showed him the box.

"A what?" he asked.

"P.G. It means Please Go!" laughed Sue and shoved Dad out the door.

After that Sue came around almost every week.

One Friday, I told her that Dad had started acting oddly.

"He's moved the furniture around and he's had his hair cut differently. He's even given his sock drawer a good sort out and bought some new clothes."

Sue said not to worry about Dad. She said it just meant he was 'getting his life back together', as she put it.

"You never know," she said, "He might even have a lady friend."

I'm afraid I laughed when she said this.

"What's so funny?" Sue said, "Your dad's still young and attractive!"

I laughed even more then, as I'd never heard the words 'Dad', 'young' and 'attractive' all in the same sentence before.

"And anyway," I said, "He loves Mum and me. He can't possibly love anyone else!"

"Aaah," Sue said, "Perhaps I need to explain to you about the elastic heart."

"The what?"

"Hearts are like elastic," said Sue, "They can easily stretch to make room to love another person."

"You mean Dad loves someone else?"

"No," said Sue. "I'm just saying that one day it could happen. It's possible."

"But he'd still love me and Mum, as well?"

"Forever!" smiled Sue.

I didn't know what to say then, so I decided not to think about it at all until I had to. Which, as it turned out, was to be sooner than I had expected.

I must have caught Dad at a weak moment for lo! a miracle occurred and Dad hired a room at the Leisure Centre for me to have my birthday party in. So I invited everyone in the class, even Smelly Jane. Both Elly's mum and Sue next door came round and offered to help Dad with the party. But Dad said no, they had done so much already and he had two or three friends from work coming to help, thank you. And when the big day arrived, that is just what happened.

Two young guys came and set up their disco lights and equipment and had us dancing in no time. And a lady called Sara was there too, helping dad put out the tables and chairs and to get the food ready. She seemed to smile at Dad an awful lot as they worked and I hadn't seen him look so happy in ages. It made me wonder if the elastic in Dad's heart was beginning to stretch.

It was a great party and in fact everything was going along swimmingly until Jane arrived. She swept into the hall wearing what can only be described as a 'frock'. At one time it must have been a bridesmaid's dress. It was bright pink and all frills, flounces and flowers. She looked like a carton of raspberry yogurt had exploded all over her. She was wearing white ankle socks with see-through sandals and her hair had been curled with tongs. Everyone turned to stare. Then Ziggy called out, "Hey Bo Peep, where's your sheep?" and Jane's happy smile slid off her face faster than ice cream off a hot spoon.

I took a deep breath and rushed up to her.

"Hiya! You look pretty," I said, as Jane rapidly scanned the room, taking in what everyone else was wearing.

"No I don't!" she said, tears forming in her eyes, "I look ridiculous!" and she turned and fled.

Unfortunately, she ran headlong into Sara, who was coming out of the kitchen with a dish of jam tarts. In the scramble, three jam tarts got stuck to the front of Jane's dress and the rest hit the floor jam side down. In one seemingly flowing action, Sara scooped the tarts off the floor and herded Jane into the kitchen and, winking at me, rather firmly shut the door behind them.

Jane and Sara emerged ten minutes later carrying the last few plates of food to the table. Jane's hair had been put up in a simple high ponytail and she was wearing Sara's thin black cardigan over her dress, which covered up the jam stains but also toned down the raspberry colour. Her eyes were still a bit red from crying but she looked happier and calmer and a lot less like Bo Peep and, more importantly, she looked like she was going to stay.

I suppose I should have thanked Sara for what she did, for without a doubt, she had saved the day as far as Jane was concerned. But there were two things that bothered me about the way she had so quietly and efficiently dealt with the situation. The first was that Dad looked so proud and thrilled with her as a result, I could hear the elastic in his heart stretching. And the second? Well, it was just the sort of thing my Mum would have done.

...but the stars started to disappear

Caroline Collingridge

The little glass ball was full of snow and water. Emily had kept her Christmas present on the windowsill for the last three months. She had never seen a snow globe before and when she got it in her Christmas stocking she fell in love with it immediately and kept shaking the globe so all the snow would float around the globe. It was magical!

It was a Christmas scene with the Three Wise Men coming to visit the baby Jesus in the manger. There was the star in the east as well as other stars, but they weren't as bright as the star in the east. She knew the Christmas story inside out and thought it was truly amazing that three men could walk all that way, thousands of miles, by just following a star. Emily had started to knit some little bootees in case the ones they were wearing in the globe got worn out from all that walking. She knew that once they had seen the little baby, they would have to walk all the way back again.

"What a dreadful thought," she mumbled to herself after having the globe for a week. "They must be so tired and hungry after such a long journey. I'm going to make new shoes for them and some cakes so that they will have something to eat on the way back." She was thinking ahead on their behalf. She was a very thoughtful child like that...always thinking about what other people might need.

It was now March and the globe was still on the window sill. It was the first thing she picked up in the morning after opening the curtains. She always looked outside, said "hello" to the garden and then she would pick up the globe, shake it and talk to the Three Wise Men. She couldn't talk to the baby as it was too young and mum and dad (she was told they were called Mary and Joseph) were too busy admiring their little one to notice her. So she focused on these three men. She loved their funny long clothes and their beards. She had never seen beards as long as the ones they were wearing. In fact, she had never seen men like that before except occasionally on TV. These men were different.

They truly seemed to be wise as their faces were smiling, despite their long walk. They looked so happy.

One morning she picked up the globe as usual but as she was looking at the familiar scene, the stars started to disappear. She couldn't believe her eyes as one by one, they were gone. Last of all was the brightest star in the east. But even that disappeared. She was so upset, she started to cry.

"What's happening? Oh dear, what are you going to do now? You won't be able to walk back. You won't have any stars to guide you. Where have the stars gone?" The more she looked, the more questions came into her mind. And the more questions she asked, the more upset she got.

Perhaps they fell onto the floor and she started scrabbling around her bedroom and under the bed looking for the stars. She couldn't find any…only dust and feathers from her pillows. She was convinced they were in the room somewhere.

Then she looked more closely at the globe and noticed that the animals were losing their fur. Then the Three Wise Men lost their funny hats. Gradually everything inside the globe started to disappear at an alarming rate until there was nothing.

By this time, Emily was so distraught that she rushed down to her mother in sobs. Her favourite Christmas present was no more! Her mother comforted her as best she could. She too was puzzled as to why everything had gone. She'd had several snow globes bought for her when she was young and this had never happened to her. As she was contemplating this, she turned the globe upside down and there on the label was written:

"Beware – this globe contains special water.
Shake it too much and everything disappears.
Nothing lasts forever.
That is the story of life!"

The Possibilities are Endless

Kathy Schilbach

So tiny. I hold you in my arms, stroke my fingertips across your cheek, and think of your future.

Maybe you'll be an architect and build bridges and skyscrapers. Or you'll be a TV weather girl and forecast frost and hurricanes. Or will you be a designer, creating toys for the super-rich? Or an MP, voted in to champion the poor?

I blink away a tear. There were complications at your birth. They say you'll have severe learning difficulties. But I look at your smile, like sunshine filling the room, filling my heart, and I think: "What do they know?"

The Turqoise Ring

Cherrie Taylor

We met by the seashore. It was early in April.

I had taken off my shoes and was running along the sand into the shallow water. I danced and kicked my feet and watched the spray cascade around me. It was early morning - the sun low and rising in the east but there was definite warmth in the air.

My mind was lost in the sensations surrounding me - the blue sky streaked with white wisps of cloud and seagulls dipping and diving above the fishing boats, as they made their way into the harbour.

I moved along the shore more slowly, enjoying the feel of the sea and salt on my skin when I heard a cry and looking up I saw a figure in one of the small boats. He was waving and shouting.

"Watch out, take care!"

I wonder who he is.

The boat drew nearer and the man jumped out pulling the boat to the jetty. I walked towards him.

He smiled. "Didn't mean to alarm you but there is a deep drop in the beach ahead."

I smiled back. "Yes, I know – thanks, though."

I was just about to walk away when he held out his hand

"I found this in the nets today. Would you like it?" He opened his hand and held up a ring. I could see the colour of the stone, a vivid opaque turquoise set in a gold band. He placed it in my hand. As I held it I felt a strong vibration. I knew at once it was Tibetan turquoise. I stood there transfixed.

His voice brought me back. "It's been in the sea a while and needs to adorn a beautiful lady's hand."

I gently eased it on to my ring finger. It fitted perfectly and I held my hand out for him to see. He looked up and our eyes met. I saw then that the colour of his eyes matched the stone - and the stone matched the sea and the sky

"It's beautiful, but shouldn't we find out if it's been lost - someone has lost it?"

He looked pensive. “Maybe…” he said, “the coast guard usually knows. If no one claims it, though, it’s yours - okay?”

I went to give him the ring but it was tight on my finger. I exaggerated a little and laughed. “Oh dear, it doesn’t want to leave me.” I offered him my hand. He held both his hands over mine and slipped the ring off my finger.

He smiled again. “I’m down here most days - depends on the tide of course - should find out in day or two.”

I watched as he pulled his boat further up the jetty. He took off his oilskin jacket and hood and pushed his hands through his hair - that thick red hair I had glimpsed earlier. He turned and waved.

Three days passed and I returned to the seashore. It was later in the day.

Wonder if I’ll see him again...will he have the ring? He had been in my mind and my thoughts had kept me awake at night. There had been storms out at sea and from my attic room I had heard the wind and the crashing of waves.

There was a gathering of fishermen by the jetty. Their boats tied together. I walked closer to them hoping to see the man, but looking from face to face - he wasn’t there.

An older man with a weathered face looked over in my direction and spoke to the others. A younger man passed him an envelope. He came towards me.

“This is for you.”

I held it for a moment then slid my hand inside and carefully opened it. There was a note and attached to it - with a white ribbon was the ring.

Beautiful mermaid of the seashore.
The ring is yours. No record of it being lost.
I hope it will bring solace for your spirit and
allow your soul to express itself once more.

My soul...how did he know?

The fishermen were looking my way. They said no more and I made no enquires.

I put the ring on my finger and touched the turquoise stone to my lips. It was even more vivid than before and I felt the healing and protection. I walked along the sand and then ran and ran, splashing and kicking the waves. I looked out towards the west. The sun was low and the sky was ablaze.

Was there a boat out there? Could I see a figure on board – the red haired man?

The ring twisted on my finger.

I held it tight and closed my eyes.

Trekking with the Toads

Christine Mustchin

She stands at a distance from the chanting voices. She shivers, chilled as much by the Italian prayers as by the cool spring air. A movement at her feet distracts her. She looks down. Close by, a toad is jumping along the gravel path of the cemetery. Instinctively she steps back and the ugly intruder hops away. At intervals it stops as if to contemplate the way ahead. She follows its progress towards the lake until it drops out of sight.

The voices reach a crescendo and she looks up to see the coffin being lowered into the ground. People are weeping now. Silent and dry-eyed, she takes her place beside her husband. When he touches her arm to leave, she reaches for his hand. He hesitates at her gesture, an uncharacteristic reluctance that she notes. They walk side by side, next to the wall of tombs, she out of step with his rhythm. And hanging heavily in the dank air, the shadow of a taciturn villager now in his grave, Alessandro's father, once as stubborn as he was strong. Kate turns her head and looks at Alessandro, sees nothing of his father in him. Worlds apart: Alessandro's a Milan office with its law books, files and computers, Piero's a mountain track at dawn, fifty village men beside him and a shotgun under his arm.

The huddle of mourners is already dispersing into the grey drizzle. Nothing more for them to mark Piero's departure to eternity. No sandwiches curling at the edges, no false bonhomie among relatives and friends last seen at another funeral perhaps or a wedding. And no drinking to excess, no sentimental toasts, no spurious speeches. How differently they mark death here in rural Italy. A notice will appear on the large board outside the commune, the little town hall opposite the main church in the village. Stark in its black lettering and obligatory black edging, it will stay there until rain has faded it or the need for another notice replaces it. There was nothing like that to mark her own father's passing: a thoroughly English farewell.

She was crying; the smell of lilies choking her. In her memory the coffin did not move. The curtains closed, the music faded, another prayer, more music, cue exit and the crying stopped. It had to. Platitudes to field, respects to acknowledge. Her father was loved by so many.

Alessandro came up to her. Their first meeting.

"My condolences," he whispered. "Sincerely. Your father was a wonderful person." He embraced her. It felt right. Everyone was looking. It still felt right.

The hint in his voice of Italian roots was like honey or cream, a balm to her. She remembered her father speaking of him as his best student, regretting his return to Italy.

"I had to be here."

"Will you come back to the house, Alessandro?"

"Of course."

"*Grazie.*" It seemed natural to choose the Italian word.

He moved aside. A black wave advanced: the white spume of outstretched hands and sorrowful faces.

"Thank you for coming."

"Please join us afterwards. You know the address?"

"So kind of you. The flowers, they're beautiful."

"Your eulogy. Thank you. I'll not forget the words."

A via crucis, a purgatory, of responses.

At the foot of the cemetery steps they stop. She turns towards Alessandro, their faces close, a faint smell of incense between them.

"Are you okay?"

He steps back. "And you?" His voice is flat, devoid of feeling.

She does not answer. She points down to the gravel path. Another toad is charting its way across the cemetery.

"Be careful where you tread, Kate," he warns. "The toads are migrating to the lake"

"I know. Down from the mountains every spring to lay their eggs in the water. You told me."

He lets go of her hand and they leave the toad to follow its own inevitable course. Maria is waiting at the top of the cemetery steps. She is staring across at the lake as if her eyes are searching for her husband's resurrection. She is the only one to dress in black. A village custom. How long does she have to wear it? Kate remembers Alessandro telling her, but not the detail. How different this from the Italy she loves. She was captivated from that very first day.

A sunny day. She turned a corner and stopped, so abruptly that an immaculately dressed Italian girl bumped into her.

"*Scusi.*"

Kate offered the apology, a sharp look the only reply.

Alessandro stopped too and pointed ahead.

She looked up.

"Magnificent," she said. "That would really be a place to get married."

"I thought you didn't want a church wedding?"

"Ah, but that…" she swept a hand towards the façade of Milan cathedral, "…would be spectacular."

"It would be just as beautiful in the village church, right on the lake."

"And keep your parents happy too, no doubt."

They walked across the piazza, a slalom course between the tourists.

"Let's find somewhere quieter," he suggested.

The café-bar was hidden down a side street, the city an elegant backdrop behind it. Their glasses of Prosecco stood untouched on the table. She wondered what to toast.

"Let's drink to Milan," she said.

They chinked glasses.

"The right decision to come here then?"

She nodded. "Great city, great job and you, of course. My Italian dream really." She paused and blocked out a childhood image of her father"s country house. "Just don't ever ask me to live in the village."

They reach the top of the cemetery steps. Together with Maria they walk, a slow trio, up the narrow tarmac which morphs into a farm track, then winds into the mountains. There will be no one waiting at the farmhouse, only the embers of the early morning fire.

Alessandro throws a log on the fire. Maria prods it, encouraging it to burn. Kate watches, but not for long, her eyes are drawn to the shotgun above the old stone fireplace. It hangs like a macabre portrait of the man now past.

"Should that be there now, Maria?" she says.

"I'll leave it be for now."

"Don't you need a permit?"

Alessandro frowns. "Not now, Kate."

"But doesn't it remind…?"

"Not now, Kate," he insists.

She shrugs and drinks her espresso. Alessandro pours himself a brandy. In the hearth the flames take hold. A smell of burning wood filters through the room. A spark bursts upwards into the chimney with a crack.

Maria stares up at the silent gun. "It'll not be used again."

"If only it hadn't been used at all." Kate keeps the thought to herself.

"I still don't understand. He was an experienced hunter. I've lost count of the wild boar he shot." Maria's words are no more than a whisper, swallowed up by the roaring fire.

"It was an accident, Mamma."

They all know that but Alessandro's words are no comfort.

"It should never have happened. He was too young to die." Maria speaks to his comfy old chair, an empty hollow full of memories.

Alessandro pours himself a second brandy. Kate crosses the room and stands behind him, drawing her fingers gently through his hair, letting the touch of her hand linger. But he will not be drawn. She leans towards him and places her mouth gently against his cheek, tasting his skin as she kisses him.

He shakes her away. "Please, Kate, not now."

She straightens up, goes over to Maria, folds her arms around Maria's plumpness, burying her face in Maria's neck, feeling the dryness of Maria's skin against her own.

"It's too late for that, Kate." There is no mistaking the reproach.

Kate steps back. She looks across at Alessandro; his eyes are still fixed on his brandy.

"I just wanted…"

"You never got on with him, Kate, why pretend now?" Her voice is brittle and full of pain.

The signs were there from the very first day. A grey autumn day welcomed her into the family home. Sitting around the farmhouse table with the unfamiliar smells and sounds and food, of course. She struggled. Her perfect Italian no match for their dialect. Her appetite no match for the hours of eating. And then Piero's question.

"When are you leaving your job?"

She winced. "I'm not."

"You mean you'll be working after the wedding?"

She turned away, looked quizzically at Alessandro. Was there something they should have discussed?

"Papà, Kate has a good career in international banking." Why did Alessandro not sound more convincing?

"And you don't mind?"

Alessandro did not reply. It was Kate who answered. "Milan's not like the village; things are different in the city."

"Doesn't seem right to me."

They rarely spoke after that.

Kate drops her arms. Maria moves closer towards the fire, staring at the flames as though that is where she belongs. Her cheeks burn red but she makes no effort to draw back from the hearth. Kate turns away. Her face is burning too from the smoldering heat, so like the sun that day when her father fell.

"My father was too young to die, too. Always off with the hunt." She spits out the words. "'It's a part of our heritage, part of our tradition,' that's what he said. Right up to the day he was thrown from his horse."

"Why do you resent what he did?" Alessandro looks up from his glass, his voice loud and unpleasant.

"Isn't it obvious? It was a complete waste of a life." It had taken the light from her mother's life too.

"Just like my father I suppose?" His voice roars across the room.

"Don't tell me you're not hurting." Kate wishes she had not shouted back.

"You don't understand do you?" Maria's voice explodes above the crackling fire. "My grandfather hunted and his father before him. Hunting was my husband's life."

"And his death." Blunt and cruel and unexpressed. Kate struggles to contain her rage.

The wood smoke begins to choke her. Its fumes envelop her like a shroud. She opens the back door on to the dying light of the day and storms out. She turns towards the woods. Her feet sink, with a slippery, silky sound, into fallen leaves and water-logged chestnut shells: remnants of a long past autumn. A branch rustles as she brushes against it. A bird call punctuates the gloomy air. She listens to the sounds, prisoners in the silence of the wood, uncanny, as old as the ages, predictable, unchanging. She longs for the silence of the city, those rare nights in London when the streets finally fall empty and silence is defined against the hum of distant traffic, or the faint footfall of people and their voices, an ever-changing score, unpredictable and yet familiar.

Along the track a cluster of small shapes approach: familiar, staccato movements. A large toad passes by her feet, its slimy gnarled skin a repulsive remnant of a past unknown and unknowable. One or two smaller toads follow. Kate shrinks away from them as they pass her by, envying them the instinctive single mindedness that takes them down to the lake. She turns away to the mass of the mountain, steep steps upwards along the track. Dark atavistic tree shapes loom out of the dusk. Shrubs brush against her. The dense undergrowth hinders her path. Her limbs are infected with the dank air, a heaviness fills her as she walks. She stops for a moment to sit on an old tree stump, dampness seeping into her clothes. Below her the lights of the farmhouse, above her nothing but wild forest. Unfamiliar noises, strange birdsong, wind whispering in the mountain pines and then the silence, an absolute silence. She closes her eyes and wishes her anger could dissolve within the total stillness of the moment. When she opens them again, she is staring at a foreign pair of eyes. Her anger falls away, replaced by rivulets of fear. She has never seen one in the flesh, only pictures enhanced by Piero's stories but there is no mistaking the creature in front of her.

She sits rigidly still, scarcely daring to breathe, terrified a sound will disturb the fragile equilibrium. The wild boar also holds its enormous body still, its eyes fixed solely on her. She hears him snort, angry animal breaths. Slowly, oh so slowly, she feels for something, anything to throw. She touches a handful of stones, she scrapes them up, launches them into the air. How far away will they land? Far enough for now. The boar turns, lumbers towards the noise. She runs. Nothing else to be done. Back down the path, back towards the farmhouse. And as she runs she hears the crashing, the boar crashing, the boar coming after her. A scream rips through the wood, her scream.

She runs on, clumsy, desperate steps. She cannot see the tree root. She trips, she falls, but feels no pain, aware only of the pulsing of blood inside her head. Her chest swells with the beat. The noise of the approaching boar invades her. She screams again exhausting her lungs. The sound dies on the wind. And as it dies, a gunshot rings out, fracturing the air. She hears the boar lumber away, then all becomes silent again. Her face sinks into the earth. She tastes the damp mud and begins to sob. Finally, finally she dares to look up. A familiar figure is standing over her, a shotgun on his arm.

She turns a soil-smeared face towards him. “I didn’t know you could use a gun.”

“It’s a family tradition.” Alessandro looks at her severely. “You could have been killed, wandering off alone like that into the mountains. I know what’s out there.”

“And I don’t, of course.”

“It’s part of my world.”

She leaves the obvious reply unspoken.

He begins to walk back to the farmhouse as she stumbles to her feet. She follows him as best she can. She sees him reach the farmhouse door. It opens. Across the path a wedge of light shines out. He turns towards it and crosses the threshold into the house. The light hangs across the path, waiting for the door to close. Kate reaches it but does not turn to enter the house. Instead she steps across the bright beam and into the dusk beyond. Behind her the door slams shut. Ahead of her, along the darkening track, the toads continue their valiant trek to the lake with enviable certitude. She hesitates, enough to focus on their disappearing shapes, then picks up their trail and follows them along the path ahead.

Today

Sandra Wood-Jones

Today is a special day for Lolita. It is the first day of the rest of her life.

Lazy on her lounger, feet up against the railing on her balcony, she patiently waits for her gentleman friend to turn up. While drawing deeply on her lipstick stained cigar, Lolita feels the warmth of the sun on her face.

The streets are quiet and trade is slow today. Catchy Salsa tunes escape from behind closed shutters of the bar next door and only the humming of a fat fly disturbs her peace. She swipes at the fly with the back of her hand and touches its wings. The fly too is drowsy and dopey from the heat.

Lolita can hear footsteps coming down the road and turns to look. It's not her friend but a member of the clergy, on his way to church. He hurriedly walks past, leaving behind an invisible cloud of disdain. Lolita doesn't give a damn. The pleasure is all hers.

Yesterday, Lolita made a momentous decision to quit.

Today, the working girl turns seventy two. She will accept her friend's proposal and become a proper Senora. Happy Birthday, Lolita.

We Never Knew

Rhona Gorringe

"I'll start up here, Robert," I said, gripping the sides of the loft ladder.

"I'm sure it's all junk, Angie," Robert warned, "Nothing's labelled but have a good root around. You know Mother kept everything. Take the lantern torch. I'll do Dad's den."

I wasn't looking forward to this. With both parents dead, Robert and I had to put their house on the market. It was too small for Robert and his family and, for me, it held too many memories.

I clambered off the top rung and the beam flickered over boxes and ghostly shapes swathed in sheets. Motes of disturbed dust danced in the pinpricks of light filtering through the rafters. I flinched as a large spider ran across one of the joists. Dense cobwebs brushed my face and a fly started a feeble buzz. The cistern gurgled noisily as if angry at the intruder. It was eerie. I propped the flashlight on a box and looked around.

As my eyes adjusted, I recognised my doll's house, Robert's first tricycle and the rocking horse we used to fight over. A toboggan, with a pair of small football boots tied to its runners, lay in one corner, familiar but now unfamiliar. They looked forlorn and neglected, reminders of carefree days when we were wrapped up in our own world.

Next to Mother's sewing machine, her tailor's dummy lolled against a box, spilling books and tattered papers; domestic accounts; our parents' passports and our school reports jumbled with some war time newspapers detailing the German advances. I felt an irritation that Mother had kept such rubbish. Then I saw the paper sewing patterns and remembered the fancy dress costumes and dolls' clothes Mother used to make for me. Tears welled up and I wanted those days again.

The dust made me cough and I lurched against a split box. A brown covered photograph album flopped out. I had never seen this before. I squatted and turned the black pages with crinkle-edged snaps of my parents

They looked incredibly young, standing with crossed racquets at a tennis club. Flicking over I saw a picture of Mother and Dad on board a ship. A large sun hat covered Mother's blonde hair and Dad had a panama. They had been keen travellers in their youth. Then I saw them in a garden I didn't recognise. I knew they had moved house frequently before we were born but never knew why.

No matter how well you think you know your parents, their courtship and life before you entered their world, it is always difficult to imagine. I felt like a voyeur but couldn't stop looking. I knew they married just before the war so these pictures must have been mid thirties.

I turned more thick pages and saw Mother and Dad, this time wearing a Tyrolean hat, standing in what looked like a castle courtyard with snowy mountains behind. Odd, I thought, I didn't remember them talking about Austria or Switzerland. There was a gap where some leaves had been torn out. Then we appeared with our dogs and rabbits. I stood in the garden in a Welsh costume mother had made for the school's Coronation parade. I remembered the feel of the starched lace-edged apron. I couldn't help my tears.

"Hey, you've been up here a long time," I jumped. "What are you doing?" Robert's fair head popped up through the hatch. "What's that you've found?"

"Look, Robert. Look at this album. Have you seen it before?" He hauled himself up and shuffled to my side.

"Well, you know Mother!" He let out a low whistle. "Gosh, you were skinny and now look at you!"

"Don't be so unkind, Robert. You were definitely chubby. Look at you in those dungarees! But this is strange, why have some pages been torn out?"

"I don't know'. Maybe they got damp or mildewed. Let's see."

I passed him the album and dislodged another box. Loose photographs fluttered out from yellowing envelopes.

"Robert!" I gasped and held out a group photograph with Dad in a military uniform with a large swastika on his sleeve. Other men wore similar uniforms and in the centre was the unmistakable figure of Adolph Hitler. Disbelief flooded through me. Silently, I passed it to Robert.

"Bloody hell! What…?" Robert gasped.

"And look, here's more! Dad couldn't have been a Nazi. Mother couldn't have supported them, could she?" I whispered, "She worked so hard for the refugees and felt so strongly that..."

Feeling a shiver, I stared at Robert.

He looked confused, "This can't be right, Angie." His lips twitched as he stretched towards the box. "Let's see the others."

"I don't want to see them," I croaked.

"But we could sell them or give them to a museum."

"What! And expose them…and us, as children of Nazi sympathisers?" Bile rose in my throat. I loved my parents and treasured their memory. "Not surprising we never heard anything about grandparents or even uncles and aunts, if there were any. They must have disowned us."

Robert's brow furrowed, just like Dad's when he was puzzled.

"I think I can put a name to some of these," he murmured, "Himmler, Goering and that could be Rommel. Where do you think these were taken?" He looked at me, "This is history, theirs and ours but such a long time ago."

"It might be history to you but not to Andrew Clark, in my class. His parents died in the blitz. His elder brother brought him and his sister up, single-handed. And there were thousands, millions like him." I took a deep breath. "A museum?" I snorted, "How can you be so heartless? We must burn them. Give them to me. Now. I'll put them in the grate." Suddenly I felt angry.

"No, I don't think we should, at least, not yet. There must be an explanation." Robert's face was pale, "Why don't you make some coffee? I'll see if there's anything else."

I wobbled down the ladder. I felt betrayed by my parents for keeping this double life from us and furious with the attitude Robert was taking. I gazed at the photograph on the sideboard of Robert and Mother watching Dad push me on the swing and wondered who had taken it. I wanted to smash it but then remembered Dad's gentle voice and warm laughter as I squealed "More, more, higher." Choking back tears I turned it face down as though it was contaminated.

I scrubbed my hands hard as if to erase what I had touched. I reached for the biscuit tin and noticed, for the first time, the faded Alpine scene swirling round it. I wanted to stamp on it. Familiar street sounds and a dog barking jerked me back to the present. I felt bewildered. I wanted to be gone from this hateful house and its secrets. But I couldn't escape the past.

I put a foot on the ladder and called to Robert. "Coffee's ready. Have you found anything?"

"Here, can you take these?" His voice was muffled, "I don't

know what the papers are. Some are in German, almost illegible but worth closer inspection." His sweater had thick whorls of cobwebs across the shoulders and his cheek was smudged. I climbed a couple of rungs and took a box and a small writing case.

Sneezing, Robert descended the ladder. He paused and raised an eyebrow at me over the photograph but said nothing. I put the case and box on the kitchen table and we divided the contents into two piles of dog-eared papers.

"You take that lot and I'll have a go at this." Robert pushed the ragged bundle towards me. I stared at the fusty flotsam and jetsam that represented my parents' life and felt lost.

Again there were household accounts. I couldn't imagine why mother had kept them. A tattered ration book was tied to a large envelope marked Dad's Papers. My eyes prickled at the sight of mother's firm hand.

"Look, here's an announcement of your birth, Angie. I forgot your middle name was Louisa. Angela Louisa Forestgate. That makes you Alf." and Robert began to laugh. I managed a smile. I didn't feel like it but it released some of my tension. "And this is their marriage certificate, March 1939, just before the war," he went on, "Mother, spinster of the parish, Joyce Muriel Bellows. She could too, when she was mad."

I felt anger rising again, "Robert, we are children of Nazi sympathisers, Jerry lovers. How can you be so flippant?"

His expression softened and he touched my hand. "I know it's grim but we've got to do it."

After some minutes of grunts and sighs, Robert looked up, "Well, there's nothing very illuminating here. It seems Dad spent some time in Vienna studying, before the war but I knew that." His fingers touched Dad's Papers. "Do you want this or shall I take it?"

"No, I've had enough of this - this mystery. Robert, what do you think it's all about?" I pushed back the chair. "This coffee's cold. I'll make some more."

I was just pouring the milk when Robert cried out. "Good heavens! I don't believe it. I just don't! This is crazy!"

I leaned over his shoulder and saw a jumble of papers, old photographs of Dad in short trousers and knee length socks, together with another boy and then some of him, older, again with this other boy. There were a couple of German newspapers. Robert tried to arrange the photographs in a chronological sequence. There were two birth certificates.

"Look, look!" he jabbed at the certificates. "Dad had a brother.

A twin judging by the dates on these certificates."

I read the looped writing, "14 April, 1914 at 4.35am. William Forestgate. Yes, that's Dad, though mother always called him Will - and what does the other one say?"

"14 April, 1914 at 6.45am. Dennis Forestgate. Registration District Chiddlestone, sub-district of Crofton. That's the Midlands isn't it?" Robert scratched his head. "Dad always said he'd like to go back one day."

"Mother wasn't keen. She said it was too far for a day." Robert nodded.

"Twins, why didn't we know? You can see the likeness, same blonde hair." His fingers curled round the photographs of two lads in hiking gear. He rolled his eyes and shook his head.

I was mystified, "I wonder what happened to him. What do the newspapers say? Your German's better than mine."

"This is July 1953. There's a small paragraph circled." Haltingly, Robert translated. "A body was found on the Munich U-Bahn U3 track, at Basler Str. early yesterday morning. He has been identified as Dennis Forestgate, an Englishman, living in Munich since 1945. My German's not good enough for the next bit but something about next of kin." Robert's face was flushed, "Hey, I think I remember Dad going away and Mother fussing about a passport and foreign money. He must have gone to Munich. Dennis must have had an accident or committed suicide, but I wonder why we were never told."

Robert rifled through more papers. They had both studied in Vienna but Dennis didn't return to the UK with Dad. We didn't know what he did. His UK ration book was cancelled. There was an undated postcard of the English Gardens, Munich and the postmark was blotched. The only German Robert could make out was "...Englent. tut mir leid. Auf Wiedersehen."

'...England. I'm sorry. Goodbye. D.'

I breathed hard and tears for my parents' sadness and Dad's loss started to fall, "I don't think those photograph are Dad at all, Robert." I murmured, "I think they're Dennis. No wonder he was never mentioned."

Mermaid

Audrey Lee

I'd had enough. My ankles were really hurting and I had to do this somersault and land on both feet. The kids were laughing their heads off and not in an entirely encouraging way. I had to get out.

I told Seb so over a coffee.

"Okay," he said, "You leave. What then?"

"Look, I'm twenty-one. The world is my oyster, mate."

"More like your frozen fish-stick. Don't do it, Jez. This is the Hot House. People fight to get in here. Anyway, you're the only one who doesn't mind me falling on top of them."

"Really?"

"It's a good life, Jez. We just don't get home much, that's all."

No wonder that was his first consideration. Seb had a partner who was a real stunner and I envied him like mad. I couldn't seem to keep a girlfriend. It was partly that we never had a Saturday night off – and partly that it was hard to look cool when my mug was permanently coloured by the dye from my red nose.

As it turned out I couldn't hand my notice in that week because Truro pulled a hamstring and I had to cover.

It was that week that I saw this girl. I was dying for some nosh so I'd slipped out to the High Street. I fancied fish'n'chips so I ended up at the usual place, a mixture of greasy spoon and oriental mystery.

Anyway, there she was, working behind the counter. She had real black skin like shiny black satin. Black isn't unusual round here of course – most people vary from coffee to chocolate – but she had something special. I suppose I thought she was beautiful but I'm not even sure of that. Gazing at her, I wasn't in a cafe in Camden anymore, I was riding a camel through the Arabian desert and being mesmerised by naked girls dancing to the music of the mysterious east - mind you, that was not surprising - the cafe played it all the time.

I was in that cafe every minute after that. I had more coffee than was good for me, but she never once raised her head in acknowledgement. I got a bit perturbed about it.

I noticed that if I went in there just before closing, this large white woman with the bossy walk would sometimes come in and order coffee, and then she and the black girl would both leave together. I was intrigued. The next time I saw this woman I sat myself down beside her and whipped out some flyers for the circus.

"Excuse me, madam," I said, "but you look like just the sort of person who might find the circus a novel, if not electrifying, experience."

She looked up, smiled, and said in a posh voice, "That sounds like fun!"

I had planned to charm her into conversation, but that was all I got.

I cornered Hep behind the bar and asked, very cool, what the black girl's name was.

"Dunno," he said. "We call her Niobe."

"Where does she come from?"

"Dunno...I know she gets the thirty-eight bus."

That was my chance. I legged it down to the bus stop and sure enough there she was. There was no time to beat about the bush so I just handed her a complimentary ticket for the next performance with *from Jez* written on it.

"Hi babe, take a walk on the wild side," I said, playing it cool. "I'll meet you after the show."

Well, that was it, and I really thought I would never see her again.

Blow me down, when I was standing in the wings counting the audience, there she was, bang in the front. Next thing I knew we were facing each other over yet another coffee.

First thing I ever heard her say was, "Thank you, Jez." She had a strong African accent and I was spellbound by the way her white teeth gleamed in her ebony face. It was a face you could never forget.

"Niobe," I said, "I want to get to know you." (I guessed she wouldn't have much small talk.)

She gave a little smile, but just sat there, silent.

"So...where do you come from?"

Her black almond eyes gazed into the distance. "Ethiopia."

My heart leaped. Desert sands...tall black Africans with spears and beaded necklaces. Apart from the romance, I knew nothing about Ethiopia except that there was bound to be a war going on.

"How long have you been here?"

"About two years."

"Do you live on your own?"

A pause. So long I thought there would be no answer at all.

"All right," I said. "Just talk. Tell me the most important thing about yourself."

I could swear she flinched, and then she stood up suddenly.

"I am so sorry. This is a mistake. We are too different." She made to go and I leant across the table and held her hand so that she couldn't.

"You must leave me alone," she said. "I am no good to you…you would never understand. Not in a million years." Then she saw my face and sat down again. "Look...I am a mermaid. You know what mermaid is – in your culture? Well, that is me. It is impossible..." And with that she walked away quickly, leaving me speechless.

I can tell you it was hard to concentrate on the evening performance. I missed Seb with the custard pie and hit Spike full in the face with it, which he did not like.

My mind began working overtime on theories to explain Niobe. I half decided that the white woman was a slave trafficker who had kidnapped her from Ethiopia. She was keeping her in a hovel and collecting her earnings. Or maybe she was a pimp, working her at the weekends. Well, you read worse in the newspapers. One thing I was sure of, she was not a mermaid. I didn't believe in them. Anyway, she had legs.

After that, Niobe disappeared from the cafe. I asked behind the bar where she had gone.

"In hospital," said Leila, who had taken over the sandwiches. "Why? "

"I'm her mate," I said. "Just want to know where she is."

"St Thomas's," said Leila. "Don't know the ward, though."

Next thing, Hep disappears and comes back with an envelope. On it is written *Jez* with a black marker. "She asked me to give this to you," he said. "I nearly forgot."

I opened it up outside the cafe. Inside was a photograph. There were three women dressed in long black burka-things with only a slit for the eyes, and it took me some time to realise that one of these women might be Niobe. So this was the culture she had come from! She was trying to show me the difference between us, and in that get-up she was right about it. But then I thought, she wears ordinary clothes now, and she's bothered with the photograph just for me. It shows she cares. I was choked.

In half an hour I was on the bus to St Thomas's. Crazy, really. I didn't know her surname or what she was in there for. All I knew was I wanted to see her.

Funny how anonymous you can be in a hospital. Everyone rushing around ignoring you. I saw a pretty woman sitting behind a desk marked Reception and found the nerve to say, "I'm looking for a black girl called Niobe."

You've got to hand it to these hospital staff. In two minutes she'd got something on the screen.

"Well, the only Niobe we've got is up on Ward 11. Gynaecological."

My legs began to shake. I wasn't used to any of this: black girls, burkas, hospitals. 'Gynaecological' frightened me to death. I followed the signs to Ward 11. What would I do if they let me see her? I had my red nose in my pocket - perhaps I could make her laugh.

I washed my hands on the alcohol scrub and opened the doors to Ward 11. There was a corridor on the other side and, blow me, walking towards me was a figure with a brief case and a bossy walk. It was the white woman from the cafe, and she must have recognised me because she was the first one to say "Hello!"

"Where's Niobe?" I said, probably a bit hostile. I still suspected her of being a trafficker.

"Just round the corner." said the woman. "She's still sedated."

I expect I looked pathetic, because she continued, "Look, let's go and have a cup of tea. Sorry! I haven't introduced myself. I'm Mary Barton – and you?"

I let her lead me as if I'd lost the will to live. She made me feel like I was driving a racing chariot with no reins - she was that sort of person. It turned out that she was not a female pimp or anything of the sort, she was a Social Worker and Niobe was one of her cases. That worried me. Had Niobe done anything wrong? I must have looked upset.

"What's happened to Niobe?" I said. "I can't find anything out!"

Mary Barton just looked at me.

"She said she was a mermaid!" I blurted out, getting a bit desperate.

"That was clever of her. Every step a mermaid takes on dry land is supposed to cause pain. You'll never get more than that out of her though. It's quite against her culture to talk about such things."

"What things?"

She looked at me sort of quizzically, as though she was weighing me up. "Look...do you care for Niobe?"

I nodded.

"In that case, I'll tell you." She put her coffee down, and there was quite a long pause. "Have you heard of FGM?"

I went cold.

"Niobe has suffered the most extreme form of circumcision. It's called infibulation. At the age of five she was held down, and in a very primitive operation most of her fleshy parts were cut away. The hole they leave is variable – hers was the size of a matchstick. It has resulted in a lifetime of pain and physical complications. The doctors are doing what they can but the damage has been done. She's one of the lucky ones..."

The canteen began to swim and I felt hot with embarrassment, but the woman would not stop. She went on and on as if she had learnt it by heart.

"You see, Jez, in her world uncircumcised women are unmarriageable, and since for most women marriage is the only option, the women have done it to their little girls for centuries. It's considered to be in their best interests. It's estimated by UNICEF that worldwide, three million girls are cut annually..."

I had to get away. I was right out of my depth and I knew it. I made up an excuse just to get out of the canteen. Poor Niobe. I couldn't face her now. To think I might have put my red nose on. Grotesque.

I never saw her again.

People said she had left the cafe but I never even checked up on it.

Looking back, I 'm ashamed I let Niobe down. But I would never have been any good for her. She was right about it being impossible. I couldn't cope with a girl who couldn't enjoy sex. It's unnatural. I couldn't give her anything to make up for it, you see, and you'd need quite a lot to make up for that. I've read some more about what happened to her since then and I can tell you, what mermaids go through is nothing in comparison.

Call me inadequate but I'm no good with unhappy girls. I like them when they're up-beat and cheerful. Seb says forget all about the black girl, stick with the circus and a nice uncomplicated girl will turn up. So that's what I'm doing.

The Gardens

Cherrie Taylor

Spring…*springtime again…where have the months gone?*

I come up here each spring, early April usually, when the daffodils climb with me up the hill - up the road that leads me north to the gardens and downs. It's cold and I feel the chill against my face as I alight from the bus and begin the ascent. Not too steep - just feels like it today – I'm tired. It's been a long winter and my heart is heavy.

That smell and the colour – the dancing heads saying, "Come this way – don't look back… just up and up." I reach the gate – its open and I walk along the path glancing at the herb garden on my left and then ahead at the crocus families sitting around the trees lining the path. The trees with bark like paper pealing off.

The horse chestnut tree – sticky buds showing says, "You here again!"

I squeeze a bud between my fingers before taking the path down to the right and to the chalk pit ahead - holding this special place like a cloak safely in his arms. I walk across the lawn and peer into the pond. No fish swimming – perhaps the cold is keeping them hidden under rocks. Tadpoles though, still in their mass of spawn are growing - no longer just dots.

I climb the steps above the cave and I'm in the rose garden – no blooms - no fragrant smell – *not yet*. Under the arbour and down the descending path the hellebores light my way and the anemones wave me on - their smiles so welcome. I sit on the seat by the Judas tree – so old now it needs a protective arm to hold it up. No flowers yet born on its branches – *I love her mystery.*

The sun sends rays of warmth, tempering the chill and I walk on breathing in the air. I circle round looking for other favourites – the handkerchief tree and the strawberry tree - so surprising that I find them each time. On the ground the snowdrops and crocuses are telling me they are nearly over but the tulips are visible - leaves pushing up and they say, "We won't be long – come back and see us soon."

I leave by the lower gate and remember times past and walk downhill into the future.

A Dog Named Useless

Patricia Feinberg Stoner

Henry Prendergast opened one eye and wondered why he felt so elated. It wasn't that he usually woke up depressed: no, working for Glenwood Publishing was still a buzz after almost 18 months - but this was an unusual level of cheerfulness for a Monday morning.

Beside him, Jeannette stirred, then turned and grinned. "It's today, chéri," she mumbled through a cloud of dark hair.

Today! Of course! Henry tumbled out of bed and raced to get to the shower first. "Auprès de ma blonde..." he bellowed tunelessly as he splashed, so that Useless, who had come up for her morning cuddle, whimpered and put her paws over her ears.

"It's off on your hols you are, my gorgeous one," he told her. Useless wagged happily. You'd think she knew she was going to France today, to meet papa for the first time. Of course, Henry told himself solemnly: in her case it would be grandpère.

The Old English Sheepdog puppy had come into their lives rather unexpectedly six months ago, in March, and immediately turned everything upside down. Owning – or, as Henry sometimes thought to himself, being owned by – a large, happy, lolloping, grinning bundle of grey and white fur certainly made life... interesting.

One of the problems with the pup was that she just loved everyone. Show her a burglar and she'd lick him to death. Show her a sheep and she'd want to play with it. She was, as Henry was wont to point out, useless. Useless as a watchdog and useless as a sheepdog. Despite Jeannette's protests: "She's got a perfectly good name of her own," the nickname stuck.

Now, after a flurry of vaccinations, a microchip and a lot of paperwork, she was the proud possessor of a Pet Passport, complete with cute photo. And today she was about to put her paw on French soil for the first time.

The trip to Morbignan la Cèbe was something they looked forward to all year. Jeannette's father, Gaston, still lived in the little village in the Languedoc where Jeannette had grown up. Every September, like homing pigeons, they returned there.

Seven hundred miles away, in Morbignan, Gaston Bergerac woke with the same sense of happy expectation as his son-in law.

Now a widower, with his four children scattered across Europe, Gaston lived a contented and resolutely independent life in the ugly, inconvenient three-story village farmhouse he moved into as a young married man in 1969.

His daily routine was almost invariable. Each morning he would walk the few steps to the boulangerie for his baguette, returning home to breakfast on his pocket-handkerchief-sized front terrace overlooking the street. From there he would look down benignly as his neighbours passed on their various errands:

“Bonjour Monsieur Bergerac.”

“Bonjour Madame Dubois.”

“Salut Gaston!”

“Salut Jean-Pierre.”

Breakfasted, with the crumbs scrupulously brushed from waistcoat and moustache, the coffee cup washed up, he would foregather in the village square with his copins – gentlemen like himself of a certain age and disposition. There under the immense plane tree, comfortably seated on the old wooden bench, its green paint cracked and peeling, they would while away a happy morning with pipes and gossip, until it was time to go home for lunch.

Today, though. Ah, today was different! Today Jeannette and her husband were coming to stay, and bringing the new baby. On the whole, Gaston approved of the fact that the baby was grey and white and fluffy rather than pink and squalling. As a grandfather of seven he was blasé about small humans, but dogs he loved.

He wondered, though, how Maître would respond to an interloper. The old hound had served him faithfully in the days when they used to go hunting. Now they were both older, man and dog preferred a stroll in the woods. There was always the hope of finding a small truffle to take home. Maître, like Gaston, was partial to a truffle omelette, and he was becoming fairly useful at nosing out these delicacies.

At last the Prendergasts’ car drew up, almost filling the tiny street. Gaston needn’t have worried about Maître’s reaction. No sooner had Useless exploded from the car, all tossing hair and flirty bum, than Maître capitulated. It was love at first sight.

Jeannette and Henry spent their first day in Morbignan settling happily into familiar routines. They took Useless on their favourite walk: down the steps behind the church and along the river bank. The little path across the river, studded with uneven stepping stones, was dry. To the left, the remains of the river lapped gently in a swathe of grasses, while to the right it lay still in tepid pools. Later in the week, as tradition demanded, they would bring their picnic down here, enjoying their cheese and saucisson mid-stream.

"I can't believe that in month or so the water will be roaring over these stones," Jeannette mused. "I must take a photo of our picnic, and then get Papa to take another one at the same spot in January, for comparison."

Henry roared with laughter. "Are you aware that you say that every time we come here in the summer?"

Turning for home, they panted up the slope through the vineyard, laughing as the village dogs rushed to pay homage to the pretty incomer. Useless preened and pouted and flirted. "Takes after her maman," Henry remarked. "A real French tart."

They stopped at the café for a pre-lunch drink. Marie Claire, the owner, greeted them delightedly. "How well you look, how you've..." she stopped just short of the comment. Jeannette was no longer a child, to be complimented on how big she had grown. "How you've been missed," she amended, rallying. Jeannette giggled – plenty of the good ol' boys in the square hadn't been so tactful.

Gaston had prepared a cassoulet in their honour, and opened a bottle of Château Rouge-Gorge. After such a feast, a siesta was the only possible option, and the afternoon passed in a pleasant, drowsy haze.

The following morning Gaston proposed a treat: a truffle-hunting expedition. Somehow they all crammed into the old man's battered Peugeot pick-up with the dogs in the back, and set off for the woods.

"Maître has become an excellent truffle hound, you'll see," said Gaston proudly. "I think I can promise you a wonderful omelette for your supper."

Maître had other ideas. All he wanted to do was show off to his new girlfriend. He darted here and there like a puppy, seeking out the most delectable smells for her enjoyment, flushing an unwary rabbit, leading her to a stream for a little refreshment.

Suddenly, Useless stiffened. Her nose came up. Her tail came up - and she ran. Within seconds she was out of sight, lost among the tall trees. Jeannette panicked. "She doesn't know these woods. She'll get lost and we'll never find her." She was almost in tears.

Gaston, who had been sulking somewhat at his hound's lack of prowess, suddenly saw a way to redeem the family honour. "Find her, Maître, good boy, find her," he commanded.

The old dog bounded into the woods. Five tense minutes passed, then came an explosion of excited barks and yelps. Following the sound, they came to a small clearing with a tall oak tree in the middle. Maitre stood wagging his tail and barking frantically. There seemed to be no sign of Useless, until they spotted a plumy tail waving from the bottom of an immense hole at the foot of the tree.

"Useless," Henry commanded. No response. "USELESS!" He used his 'I really mean it' tone of voice. Slowly the tail dipped. Slowly, reluctantly the puppy backed out of the exciting hole.

"She has something in her mouth," said Gaston. And then, with a gasp, "Mon dieu!"

Proudly the pup laid her trophy at her master's feet. It was black. It was the size of an orange. Even from a distance it gave out a pungent, earthy smell. Gaston bent and picked it up.

"It must weigh almost half a kilo," he said with awe in his voice. "Do you realise, this truffle could fetch anything up to €500 on the open market?"

"Truffle?" Henry Prendergast was bewildered. "I thought they only grew in the Périgord."

Gaston regarded him indignantly. "Not at all, you English philistine. Some of the finest truffles come from the Languedoc."

There was a gleam of triumph in Jeannette's eye as she turned to her husband. "So? Do you still think she's useless?"

"Not at all," said Henry. He bent to ruffle the dog's silky ears. "What a clever girl you are," he said.

Later that evening, the family relaxed on the terrace. With a fragrant omelette aux truffes and a bottle of the excellent local white wine inside them, they were in mellow mood. It was what the French called l'heure bleue, that languorous half-hour after the setting of the sun. The swifts, which had been shrieking their heads off, dive-bombing round the church tower like demented stukas, were at last settling to roost.

The first bats fluttered out into the blue dusk.

Smiling lazily over at Useless, who lay entwined with Maître in a fluffy heap, Henry remarked: "You know, it's time we found a proper name for her. We can't go on calling her Useless for the rest of her life."

"I know," replied Jeannette, "but her kennel name, 'Silverleaf

Daddy's Delight', is just too awful."

"Why not call her after a famous huntress, like Diana," Gaston chipped in. "After her prowess in the truffle woods she deserves such a name." Jeannette pulled a face. "Oh, Papa, you know I hate human names on animals." She paused, then inspiration struck: "Of course, we could call her Artemis, it's the same thing, only in Greek."

"Yes," added her husband enthusiastically, "and then we can call her Missy for short."

Jeannette shot him a look, and he subsided.

And to this very day, whenever an unsuspecting friend asks why their pretty dog has such an unusual name, Henry and Jeannette exchange a glance. "Well," one of them will begin, "it's like this…"

Can Buy Me Love

Sue Ajax-Lewis

The Beatles sang "Money Can't Buy Me Love".
When Peter went to Riverview, he found that they were wrong.

Peter was nervous. A first meeting was always fraught with worries about making good impressions and wondering if a long term relationship was going to result. They would spend the afternoon together and see how it went.

He had been so lonely without Sally; she was irreplaceable. Sharing his life with another had seemed an impossible task. One he shrank from contemplating for a long time.

But she wouldn't have wanted him to be lonely and unhappy; she had loved him too much. He could almost sense her approval as he began to read the small ads and look online. Finally, plucking up the courage, he had made an appointment.

Peter pulled in at the gate marked Riverview Rescue and as he got out of his car, heard barking and saw a cheerful looking girl being pulled along by a large scruffy dog. He smiled and above the barking called "I'm looking for Helen."

The girl pointed to the side of the long low building and shouted "Reception's over there," as she was towed past.

Inside, Peter paused at the counter and pinged the bell for attention. A harassed pleasant looking middle aged woman in jeans came from the office area but managed a kind smile at him as she said "You must be Mr. Johnson?"

"Come to meet Polly," Peter confirmed. "I'm a bit nervous."

The woman held out her hand and said "I'm Helen, the manager. Don't worry. Everyone is, at first. Polly's a lovely girl. As you know, she's still young so she might be a bit boisterous to start with but that's only because she's glad to be getting out of the kennel. We're short-handed today. One of the girls has called in sick so we're a bit behind. Normally we would have walked her before you arrived but I'm afraid we haven't had time. She'll settle very quickly though. Come this way. You've had dogs before haven't you? I know you passed the home check and normally I would have read your file before you arrived but," she gave a little shrug, "But I didn't get chance."

She led Peter into a small side room off Reception and said "If you wait here, I'll go and get her. It's best to take her out of the kennel environment away from the other dogs because they all get so overexcited when they see someone new. They all think they're going to get adopted and we don't like seeing them disappointed.'"

Peter sat down and looked around the room. It was filled with happy photos of previous inmates and their new owners. He heard the excited scratching of claws on the lino and then Polly exploded into the room, Helen trying to calm her down. She ran straight over to Peter and jumped on his lap and began to lick his face, wagging her tail and wriggling in his arms. She had been described as a medium size terrier mix, white and fluffy, found abandoned by the dog warden. Peter felt a pang when he realised how like Sally she was - but then he knew that already because he had picked her from a photograph.

Helen watched them for a moment and then said "Take her for a walk and she'll calm down."

Peter and Polly circled the field but she didn't calm down. He sat down and talked to her but she was much too excited to be out to take much notice of him and too interested in the countryside smells and looking for rabbits.

Peter knew in his heart of hearts that she should be homed with a family with children she could play with. His life would be too quiet for her. It wouldn't be fair.

He stayed walking with her for nearly an hour, just so that she would get some extra freedom before returning to Riverview. Helen saw them coming, saw the look on Peter's face and wasn't surprised. She could have told him, from long experience, that he would come to that conclusion but she knew he had to find out for himself and after all, Polly had had a longer walk than usual.

He was just about to hand her over when a car drove into the yard and a young boy jumped out. He saw Polly and ran over to her immediately, shouting "Dad, Dad, come and look at this dog!"

Polly seemed to like him straight away, jumping around him and licking his face as he knelt down, laughing and stroking her. "Charlie!" called a man getting out of the car with his wife, "Leave that dog alone; she belongs to that gentleman."

"She doesn't actually," said Peter, "I'm just - just walking her.

Her name's Polly," he added to the boy who was now sitting beside Polly, who had rolled over on her back, waving her paws and encouraging him to tickle her tummy. "She seems to like you."

"Dad, Dad, can we have Polly please?" begged the boy, eyes shining.

Helen picked up the lead. "I'm going to put Polly back in her kennel and then give you an application form to fill in, OK?" she said, smiling at the family, and then to Peter, "Can you wait here for a few moments, then we can have a quick chat about the sort of dog that would be more suitable for you? You're an ideal person; I'd like you to have one from here."

Peter leant on his car, waiting for Helen to come back. Perhaps he shouldn't have another dog yet. Perhaps it was still too soon. Perhaps he should wait a bit longer?

Another car spun into the yard, too fast and parked next to him. A man, rather overweight and a bit scruffy, jumped out, opened the tailgate and threw out a dog bed.

A woman was staring out of the passenger window. She saw Peter and looked away.

The man shouted at him "You take unwanted dogs here don't you?" and without waiting for an answer, reached back into the tailgate and dragged out a cowering, thin rather plain black dog. It looked like a lurcher.

He pulled it across to Peter and said "Mother-in-law died. We don't want it."

He thrust the lead at Peter, "Here."

Peter started to say "But I don't work..." but the man turned away back to the car and drove it out of the yard as rapidly as he had arrived.

Peter stood holding the lead. The dog was trembling and frightened, tail clamped between her legs. She watched the car disappear and then crawled into the hard bare plastic bed, the only thing she had left in the whole world, and hid her face.

Peter had always thought of himself as a mild man but he was suddenly gripped by an intense rage.

He knelt down and spoke quietly to the dog, stroking her gently and when that didn't stop the shaking and trembling, he gathered her into his arms. He laid his face against her head and felt the tears running down his cheeks.

That was the sight that Helen saw when she came back and she understood it immediately. Peter looked up with wet cheeks.

"How can people do it?" he asked, "Not even her name."

"People do. You'd be surprised. Some people just tie them on the gate overnight. I'll take her in and process her." She held out her hand for the lead.

Peter said "Can I just sit in your office with her till she stops trembling?"

Helen nodded. "That would be a very nice thing to do for her if you have time. Thank you."

Peter smiled sadly, "Too much time now," he said. "Lots of it."

Peter sat in the Riverview office with his arms full of black dog. Calmed by the warmth and comfort of his embrace and voice but still trembling, she had dared to glance at his face and he had seen sad gentle eyes in a greying face and loved her immediately.

When Helen came back, Peter heard himself say "Can I have her?"

"Well, we'll have to officially admit her and check her over first. She won't be ready for adoption just yet. But you're upset at how she arrived. Take a few days to think about it. She won't go to anyone else in the meantime."

"I don't need to think about it. I want her - please."

"Come back on Wednesday and take her for a walk. Just to be sure."

Peter didn't want to let the black dog go. With reluctance he put her down.

But he kept one hand on her head as he said to her, "I have to go away now, Cindy, but I will come back for you and you'll never be alone or cold or hungry ever again and I will always love you."

She dared to steal another glance at Peter and something passed between them.

He looked up at Helen, "Her name's Cindy now."

Helen felt tears in her eyes. This bereft middle aged man and this abandoned middle aged dog clearly needed each other. He was obviously lonely and needed a dog to walk and care for as he was retired. "Too much time," he had said, "Lots of it."

An idea came to her. "Mr. Johnson..."

"Peter."

"Peter, if you're ever finding yourself at a loose end, I don't suppose you'd consider coming here for a few hours and sitting on Reception? That would free up the staff to spend more time with the dogs. We always need volunteers but we can only pay you with biscuits and coffee." She smiled hopefully at him. "Would you think about it."

"I don't need to think about it," Peter said again, "I'd love to. But what about Cindy? I don't want to leave her on her own."

"Bring her with you; she can be an office dog. I imagine as long as she's warm and somewhere near you, she'll be happy."

"Shall I start on Wednesday then? I could take Cindy out and then you could show me the ropes."

Helen held out her hand. "Let's do that. Welcome aboard." She looked at her watch. "Peter, I'm sorry but I really must take her in now. The dog warden will be here shortly and he's usually got more dogs for us.'"

Peter hugged Cindy one last time and said "I will come back for you," and handed her lead to Helen. "Till Wednesday then."

He peeled off his sweater. "Can you put this in her bed to remind her of me so she knows I'm coming back for her?"

Helen gazed fully at him and said "You are such a nice man. I wish all our adopters were like you."

Peter gazed fully back, only he was rather pink. "I'll be back on Wednesday then," he said again and leaned over to stroke Cindy one last time to cover his embarrassment.

As he drove away, he was making mental notes of what to buy for her. A new bed for a start although he bet it wouldn't be long before she was sharing his. Collar, lead, bowls, food, herbal supplements to build her up and make her coat shine, chews, treats, toys, a warm coat for winter...

Peter smiled joyfully; now he had a dog again and a part time job helping other dogs.

He felt happy for the first time in a long while. And he would take along a nice chocolate cake for when they had their coffee. Oh, he had forgotten to ask Helen about the adoption fee. He could pay that on Wednesday.

The radio, on low, was playing oldies from the sixties. Peter liked that because he knew most of the words. He sang along softly to the Beatles *Money Can't Buy Me Love*. And then he thought about Cindy.

"You're wrong you know," he said to John Lennon, "It can. It most certainly can."

Our Best Friend Buster

John Falconer

Dogs, particularly smaller dogs, have been a feature in the lives of our family. My cousin's family had a small brown and white terrier called Ben. When my parents were younger and before they married both their respective families had dogs and in my mother's case they had a dog and a cat both of which were strays and seemed to adopt my grandparents. For a while my parents talked about having a dog but in my father's words "If we had one it had to be high off the ground and not just grubbing along or the yappy type." My father had now set the ground rules. Although a dog is a commitment, they are generally good company and provide some security.

I never thought the idea of having a dog would catch on. Our parents, like others, mentioned various things, but for much of the time it was just pie in the sky. As a family living in Surrey, we enjoyed visiting nearby places by car and among them, but not far away, were Box Hill and Ranmore Common. There is always an abundance of dogs enjoying their walks on the open spaces.

At the time, I was still at boarding school, but on some weekends we were allowed to return to our homes. One particular weekend when I arrived home I was greeted by the family but also by a little soft brown ball of fluff. My mother and sister had recently been in touch with a Labrador breeder in Hertfordshire. They had only picked up our little friend after he had had his injections. He was an adorable little fellow who made little whimpering noises in the house going up the hall. He had long legs but they were not fully developed and he was unable to get the full use of them. We called him Buster and on one occasion he partly destroyed one of my father's hats! All the family helped with the training of Buster but my sister did most of it. While he was so young there were a few puddles on the kitchen floor to mop up first thing in the morning – not a pretty sight! Buster had his own space in the kitchen where we had a coal burning boiler which kept him warm on cold nights. We wrapped him up in a blanket like a baby every night. When the longer days in Spring arrived he started to make slight barking noises especially in the early mornings when he felt all the family should be up!

As the dog got older and his body became bigger, with his athletic legs and a real strong bark he was now starting to mature. He became a real family pooch and liked people and children. When there was a caller at our front door he would bark furiously and race up to the door. He had a very strong and large neck and with his special dog chain it was as much as we could do to hold him back. When a member of the family returned home, Buster raced round to bring them a present. This could be anything from coal out of the coal bucket or a magazine or newspaper off one of the low tables. If there was anything in his flight path this would get knocked over with a strong flick of his tail.

On one occasion after I got my car, my sister and I travelled down to Worthing taking Buster with us to visit our grandmother. When we got there we took him on the seafront for a walk. I left both of them to get a couple of ice creams and while I was away I could just see the dog wandering around on his own. He very quickly returned to my sister sitting on the beach and put his head on her shoulder. A man passing by said "We know whose dog he is!"

In his early years, we took Buster for walks in Richmond Park. Like all dogs, Buster liked being free from his lead and free to roam and looked forward to his dinner every day around 5.30p.m. He did have a few biscuits in his bowl if he was hungry and from the terrible crunching sound he made you knew he was enjoying his biscuits.

However, Buster's main enjoyment stemmed from travelling in the car from the time when he was a puppy. As soon as he heard the car engine start he was up and ready to go. To him, a walk wasn't a walk until he had been in the car and travelled to a destination. He literally travelled for miles on the back seat of the car. There were times when I travelled alone and from an outward appearance the car looked just like any other – car and driver. If we had been travelling for a while the dog used to get up, stretch his legs and rest his head on the back seat and glare at other cars. Other drivers seemed amazed that such a large dog was in the back and some used to taunt him and I could see from my car's interior mirror that his ears were raised and he was eager to get out of the car and have a go at the drivers.

Like all dogs, Buster liked to play with a ball in our garden and liked chasing cats if they were in his garden. On the whole he usually took no notice of them when going for a walk but sometimes, late at night, I took him round the roads and if he saw a cat on a wall he would bark furiously at it, disturbing the neighbours.

After some ten years or so our wonderful dog Buster was now feeling his age. He found it difficult to walk and everything was becoming an effort. One morning he was unable to get out of his bed and my father took him to the vet and that, unfortunately, was the last we saw of our dear Buster. He had been a really good friend and company and our life would now be very different without him. We certainly missed him and all the fun and enjoyment he gave us. Labradors are certainly a special breed of dog.

PART THREE

POETRY

Have you ever...

Lyn C. Jennings

Have you seen
a darkened sea
with a rippled lake
of silver at its heart
pooled by the sun
poised at the edge
of a smudge of cloud?

Have you watched
sleek-bodied sea birds
flying into the wind
wide wings out spread,
        transfixed like a painting
on the stormy skies?

Have you smelt
the rough raw odour
of seaweed, green
brown and black
layering the rocks
in a gleaming plastic coat
or felt it wrap around
your legs in the sea
like satin ribbons?

Have you touched
the rosy centre of
a sea anemone and
felt the slight sucking
as its thread-like tentacles
close your fingers round?

Have you felt
the tickle of tiny
see-through crabs
sidestepping into your hand,
or disturbed
shoals of minute
flickering fish
in clear green pools?

Have you ever gazed
so long at the setting sun
that when you turned away
            your whole world
was edged with gold?

Raising the Bowman

Rose Bray

If her father had not fancied mushrooms for breakfast,
she would not have gone into the woods
to forage for the pink gilled treats
between the fallen trees.

If the early sun had not been shining
on the clearing where she knelt,
the archer may not have seen
her simple grace
and sought her hand in marriage
and she would not have borne his son.

If he had not been middle aged
he may not have been so patient with the child,
making a small bow for his play
as soon as he could walk,
bending, shaping each yew branch
as he outgrew the other.

If the boy had not grown so tall
and become a master bowman,
he would not have been a chosen one
to serve on Henry's flagship.

His mother would not have stood on Portsmouth's Hard
waving off her firstborn son
as the Mary Rose sailed on the morning tide.
She could not have guessed,
amongst the nit combs, the wooden bowls
beside his scattered arrows,
her son would lie
five hundred years
rocked gently on his bed of sand.

It's Not Cricket, It's a Scorpion

Dave Simpson

(A small girl overheard in a doctor's surgery)

Angel of the sting, black shoe polish shine,
you're a child's threaded beads who self-starts
their own connections. Here's your at an angle
run up to the wicket: watch the birdie;
over comes the sting in the tail, a leg break.

Who can play that? And you'll catch everything
at short leg in those clutcher claws. I love
the casual edge to your close of play press
conference, how you pause, then deliver
a second killer answer no-one can wriggle
away from. But your excuse for the tail end
is a disappointment; I'd want something
rounded, sensual, less defensive-minded.

Yes I know inside there's a wholesome array
of wires, fuses, tubes, even squashy lumps.

But what'll we do when we find your follow through
on Mars, my one crunch granola with hating breath?

It Couldn't Happen Here...

Cherrie Taylor

I can hear them coming
No that's the wind
They're not here yet, not yet.

The power was down.
We had known for weeks
We'll stay, I sighed. We'll stay.

I didn't know we'd all be leaving
that the *Barbarians* would come -
it couldn't happen here...

We'd watched others pass by…
It's only a matter of time,
It's only a matter of time.

But it doesn't happen here
I heard you say over and over
again - over and over again.

It will be fine, we'll be fine-
pack our clothes and photos
put them in plastic – plastic bags.

Put your teddies in your school bags
Shall we wear our arm bands?
And bring our blow up crocodile?

How many are leaving?
Our street and all the streets
down to the sea.

It doesn’t happen here…
Come, come, quick, quick -
the *Barbarians* are coming

We spill our way
like hundreds and thousands
to the shore
to the jetty
and wait.

Scarecrows

Derek Eastwoord

Late summer sultry sun layers hazy glaze
over fields of harvested maize
and shadows lie long
making tall of the short

Now is the time
now is that time

The time of the gathering
when day's work is done
workers are gone
and all are gone home

They come from far fields
skipping light unnoticed
to the clearing
straw stuffed rags

One dances while another plays
unstringed banjo
another bangs a bodhran
and another sits and sways

But if you wandered by
you would see nothing
hear nothing
smell nothing

Just something brushing past
like a breath of wind
a strange sense of something there
cold shuddering

Muscovies

Richard Buxton

In the stable, beneath the glare of the hanging bulb,
my young feathered flock,
my responsibility, crowd the corner.
Father sits on a bale, holding the secateurs,
testing this smallest son in oversized boots.
I single out one from twenty-four.
The duck freezes, watches me with a dinosaur eye.
I catch it and clamp its folded strength.

A wing is stretched against resisting tendons
and the duck softly laments,
like a broken bicycle horn.
Proud feathers slowly separate.
We three, close together, find a new point
of balance, a shared serenity.
Father cuts with care, as if pruning a prize rose.
And I imagine him a boy,
learning from a great duck master
who went before. 'One wing will do.'
I drop the lonely lame duck outside,
and Godlike, collect another.

All done and my flock secure,
we come out into the sunlight,
our valley above and below us.
The Muscovies mill on the steep lawn,
whispering revolt, then hurl themselves
from the slope. Most, for the first time,
miss the ground altogether.
They gather, strafe us with joyful squeaks,
circle higher and higher, then,
in an unrehearsed V for victory,
disappear south, over the Graig.

I look at my father. He sniffs an apology,
stretches his face in humour, lets me share
in the secret incompetence of men;
it's only a matter of degree.
Our product is the same but we are rebalanced.
He is smaller, I am taller.
I ponder my losses, reassess my assets;
four Muscovies and a father,
all clipped.

Three Seasons of War in Four Trios

Liz Eastwood

AUTUMN

I wake	grey stone rests on my aching chest
I rise	autumn leaves stir me sideways through
I dress	put on bra pants your combat vest
I wake	grey stone rests on my aching chest
I press	messages next still no tweet or text
I call	your cell phone feel so sad and all alone
I wake	grey stone rests on my aching chest
I rise	autumn leaves stir me sideways through

DESERT FIRE

Military scarf	hides your head and face
Yellow sand dunes	striped with tanks and guns
Military force	collides in time and place
Military scarf	hides your head and face
Bullets whisper	of desert bones no mercy in fly zones
Fellow squaddies	squeeze your hand burning hell in fiery sand
Military scarf	hides your head and face
Yellow sand dunes	stride with tanks and guns

WINTER

I wake	lift grey stone from my frozen heart
I rise	winter snow stirs me sideways through
I dress you	put on your pants change blood stained vest
I wake	lift grey stone from my frozen heart
I dress	your wound next still no kiss or sex
I recall	one passionate night of love in candlelight
I wake	lift grey stone from my frozen heart
I rise	winter snow stirs me sideways through

SPRING

My long black hair	hides your head and face
Soft hands caress	scars on your back and front
Our gorgeous kisses	collide in time and place
My long black hair	hides your head and face
My heart whispers	of eternal love no despair sweet peace dove
My love I'm here	to hold your hand hope your new legs stand
I wake	I crush you close, my limbless man of steel
I rise	spring flowers stir me sideways through

Terzanelle - A Windswept Soul

Terry Westwood

It's the power of words that cause you pain
Battered by the winds of everyday life
So much to lose, so much to gain

Where has love gone, if it gives you strife
A hard brittle shell encloses our being
Battered by the winds of everyday life

The tears dry up with too much seeing
It might be bright but the glooms within
A hard brittle shell encloses our being

We enter into purgatory to confront our sin
Our mind slices life into digestible pieces
It might be bright but the glooms within

Nature takes distance but won't release us
Seeing others through a windswept soul
my mind slices life into digestible pieces

When locked inside you need a way out
It's the power of words that cause you pain
Seeing others through a windswept soul
So much to lose, so much to gain.

Pebble

Audrey Lee

Pebble
She's a rebel
Wallowing in the sand like a crestfallen bagel.
One minute solid, a rock of St. Peter,
The next all sodden, half hidden in the water.

Wobble
In the puddle
She's such a mixed up kid, she's all in a muddle.
Rolling around being something she's not
She's wasting her time. I say, "Keep what yer got!"

Scribble
In the middle
What you really are, it's not a big riddle.
You're just a simple pebble in an ocean of sand
One day you'll diminish to a dot in my hand!

I Wish I'd Married A Billionaire

Cherrie Taylor

I would design a new face, new legs
to walk the walk
beside you with full protection – a team
of guards and guns.
I would put up with your style your guile
your disrespect
for all who came before. I'd shore you up
when you tire, when you tilt.
I would admire you with a wink and deny
all they say about your past.
Of course you joke and make fun at
everyone who is not like you.
Not White. Not White. Not right.
I'd say he's kind - he's a joker
he doesn't mean what he says,
he won't do this and that - it's all a load o' shite.
And if he does I shall smile and beguile the crowd.
Enjoy my life. Put aside any principles I never had.
(Or if I did I will forget who or what they were)
I'd be so pleased - so thrilled to take your arm,
to sleep beside you (if I must)
And when the term is over
(as over it will be in four years time) …
I will shore you up when you tire, when you tilt,
give a smile and deny everything you've done.

It's win win for me.

We've won.

My Son, Our Boy

Paul Doran

I did everything I could
We both did
Did what we thought we should do
Did what we'd wished had been done for us

He never wanted for anything
He was the best of sons
We congratulated ourselves
What a good job we'd done

But something changed
Not suddenly, or we'd have noticed, we're sure
No longer appreciative, listening, seeking advice
No longer feeling the need to explain

We tried to talk as always
He was unresponsive
"It's just his age" said my wife, and I agreed
But we were wrong

From fourteen he stayed in his room a lot
When he went out we knew not where
His eating habits changed
He lost weight and his energy

And one night he didn't come home
And he didn't come home after that
He became a missing person, a statistic
My son, our boy

We anguished, we prayed
We questioned
We still wonder where we went wrong
And still we hope.

Daddy's Gone

Alexander Medwell

Kids,
Where has daddy gone?
You called for him
and he would come.
You walked with him
and held his hand.
He taught you stuff
you'd understand.
You shared with him
your love of games.
Now daddy's gone
it's not the same.

Mummy,
Why has daddy gone?
They're yours and his
daughter and son.
He cut their cords
when you gave birth.
He promised to
give them the earth.
But they are lost
inside their screens.
Now daddy's gone
out of their scene.

Daddy,
So what have you done?
Who is this stranger
you've become?
You worked too hard
and blamed the stress.
You loved them more
but seemed like less.

You can't regain
quite what you had.
Now daddy's gone
and you're just... Dad.

Cross Rail Dig

Lyn C. Jennings

A scatter of orange-clad archaeology birds
like bright patches on a dark tapestry,
peck at the red brown soil, they
scratch the constant itch of curiosity,
peeling away earthy cradles of a long-time
sleeping people, disturbing crumbling bones
with subtle knowing hands, gently lifting
them from their dreamless slumber.

They reassemble bones of
a young woman who died in the plague,
her brittle pelvic cave never having
housed a child, an innocent victim,
caught in an unrelenting cycle
of death and disease.

They expose, the broken bones
of a man of substance, whose wealth bought
him no more years than the pauper beside him,
but ensured his place in the narrative
of his descendants for generations.

The bleak earth of now uncovered
Bedlam cemetery houses the
remains of hapless victims
of fire and plague
bodies stacked
unceremoniously
like broken dolls
one upon the other.

Pacing in the shadows -
protective gear bright against
the rubble strewn ground -
workmen wait impatient
to set the great drills in motion
that will slice through all this
layered history like
giant mechanised moles
burrowing a vast web of tunnels
deep beneath the city streets,
yet when a box of bones
is carried past
they solemnly
doff their helmets.

Nineteen Forty-Five

Audrey Lee

One morning Uncle Charlie just walked in
He brought us sweets and bags of broken biscuits.
The first real laugh mum had in years, Uncle Charlie did it
fencing with the bread knife a la Errol Flynn

He took us for a treat to Streatham Odeon.
We saw Sonja Heine skating. What a wonder!
I just could not believe she was a real human being
a woman made of flesh and blood, like mum.

Going home the black-out was the pitchest black.
Uncle Charlie shone a torch and whistled.
We clung to him like drowning sailors, mum relieved and glad.
He always seemed to be there after that.

But nothing stays the same. One day along our street
a quiet house was shouting flags and flowers.
A home-made banner, wobbly with the lightness of its message
read 'Welcome home at last, our darling Pete.'

With something of a lurch I knew that soon we'd see my dad.
I wanted mum to help me make a banner.
Mum looked at Uncle Charlie and he nodded, yes, we should,
but suddenly his face was old and sad

because he knew he was a secret, a bad thing we should never
talk about, or cling to in the dark.
We put the flags out bravely but with Uncle Charlie gone
I knew the fun had left the house for ever.

Dad came home, a stranger half remembered, an exam
that needed more revision, sheer hard work.
He had 'nerves' that made him shout. "It isn't you that it's about
He's a broken man" she said. And now I'm

angry with myself for wishing Uncle Charlie back
still guilty with the weight of words unsaid
heavy with the happiness and damage of those years
that wedged the war between me and my dad.

To Alex Peckham

Audrey Lee

TO ALEX PECKHAM on his glass resin boat, lit from within (displayed at Sussex Art College, 2013)

Your installation – Interstice – has set itself up
in my brain, which is not adequate.

You've knocked the rhyme and rhythm from my words
a double whammy in astonishment.

You've sonified the human genome – Wow!
What I heard was like the muffled ping of

giant outer-space elastic bands – wonderful - but
could have been the clever use of syrup tins

for all I know. Light and sound pulsated
with your brilliance. Oh my god, I am an

empty vessel. Admiration leaks out from
my two short planks. All I know of boats

is sinking. All my painted boats have teetered
MGM style on the edge of kitsch.

Your vessel's full, thunders hidden meaning
shouts its deep dimensions, which I cannot fathom

It's the real thing – beautiful - a worn-out word.
Art without a single cliché. No short cuts

gave you any early nights. I am in awe
of those invisible two hundred plaster tiles

that kept you up. You say interaction is
more meaningful when nuanced and controlled

and that we must move carefully inside
the space, which is quite dark and dangerous:

I moved round with ease, controlled and interacting...
cresting waves of light and sound and darkness

Homefield Park

Laurie Morris

There's a boy on air - one of several bicycle daredevils, leaping into nothingness.

On landing, his friends give a muffled cheer. Meanwhile, on a court behind high chicken wire, two tanned men in white shorts sweat and grunt in their own private Wimbledon.

To the poc-poc of summer racquets,

I walk the shady path. Past the first bench where an old man catches his breath. At his feet, his spaniel licks its paw, pulls at its claws with its teeth.

I wonder, is the cafe open? Best

takeaway tea there is and always cheery! I carry my lidded cup to a bench beneath the fairy hill and sip. To my left, children shriek and swing, watched by anxious mothers, an occasional dad or boyfriend, chatting.

Two tall youths play basketball heroes, aiming at a high-stalked net, while a teenage girl sulks in the iron shelter, texting, swinging one foot.

Gets up and stomps across the field-

straight through the practice footballers, avoiding the black and white collie dog chasing a bouncing yellow ball.

My tea finished, I start for

home, past the skaters' cage. Are these dangerous animals? More like some circus species. At the tall pine, I'm met by any inquisitive squirrel: Any nuts? Sorry, not today. At the gates, I pause to look and listen, sniff the air, before leaving the park's charmed circle.

The Monthly Test

Dave Simpson

Five minutes to my monthly hospital blood test
and I'd give anything for a Kit Kat;
three minutes, even a Blue Riband would do
now Wagon Wheels are Lego car tyre size.

My number's buzzed and I'm in a cubicle
ready to roll up my sleeve. A phlebotomist checks
my name before she says, "Sharp scratch" and the needle's into
avocado pear and I'm exotic fruit - sapodilla,

rambutan or persimmon - and my thumb presses
a dab of cotton wool. Until she sees a leak;
"You've bled." A stain blots then flowers.
"My arm's empty and needs some chocolate," I say

watching her press firmly on the crook of my arm.
"Does this always happen?" "Sometimes. It's changeable,
Penguin biscuits often work." I want to itch or scratch
but go to words for wriggle – squirm, twist, twiddle.

She counts under her breath. I've moved back to
Breakaway, Mint Yo Yo; she's up to four
before I see newspaper headlines; 'Sudden Death,
Living Death, Put to Death.' Then she says, "Oh."

And there's a blood on cotton wool jammy dodger.
That doesn't count. "You've stopped. There'll be a bruise."
She stretches tape tight across marshmallow white
soft cotton wool. Hobnobs are chocolate coated

and don't forget Bourbons. She writes my name on four phials,
Chocolate Orange Club to roll my sleeve back down,
not forgetting Chocolate Digestives to pull back
the curtain and find your face in the crowded room

where you smile, "Alright?" "Yes." I've reached sultana
cookies from picnics, like those we eat at Camber Sands
after you swim with the girls in a flat October sea
and the car's salty warmth makes us sleepy.

You help me with my coat, and the cotton wool
snags against my shirt when I push my arm down the sleeve
We hold hands on our walk towards the stairs
you say, "Coffee?" Americano, latte, espresso.

Miscarriage

Alison Batcock

One frosty February day
as the first crocus bloomed,
I miscarried. Surgeons ended
the agony, neatly, hygienically.
Suddenly it was gone,
as if it had never been.
A foetus, not a child.
I never had the chance to hold
my baby in my arms.
I was drowning
in a whirlpool of sorrow,
forever sinking
not reaching the bottom.

The nursery stood unused,
cot and cuddly toys,
half-knitted matinee jacket
discarded in one corner.
My only certainty
was loss.

Years later, that void
remains. Was this the son
I never had?
I shall never know.
My eldest must take his place
unknown
beside my daughters.

A Prayer for the World in 2017 for All Faiths

Caroline Collingridge

Where there is war, let there be peace
Where there is misunderstanding, let there be enlightenment
Where there is cruelty, let there be kindness
Where there is fear, let there be courage
Where there is bitterness, let there be forgiveness
Where there is doubt, let there be Faith
Where there is loneliness, let there be friendship
Where there is loss, let there be support
Where there is illness, let there be recovery
Where there is worry, let there be reassurance
Where there is hopelessness, let there be hope
Where there is hunger, let there be food
Where there are strangers, let there be welcome
And for all – let there be love.

Seven-Seven

Wendy Green

For the fiftieth time I see the same news
With the same views of the injured travellers
Shocked by the acts of terror

But by the fiftieth time I see the same guy
With the same eye and the same man with the same smashed head
With the same blood on his same chest, stepping from the same ambulance
Into the same wheelchair and the same nurse
Pumping the same heart of the same victim
I'm shocked...that I am starting to become...comfortably numb

Even as reporters speak from the same spots
The same shots are seen on the split screen
And I want to shout "Stop ...there are children watching
Stop ...there are friends and relatives watching"
And later still "Stop ...the victims are watching themselves
On the evening re-run re-run"
These are real people not actors

Another view another train . . . so
To refocus my brain I watch Emmerdale
The relief is immense and I'm no longer tense when my friend arrives
But I need to hold on to the fictional reality
I need to remember the beauty of nature so I set the tape
For Hampton Court Flower Show
But when my friend leaves I find programme times were changed
And I've taped the last two minutes of Hampton Court

And instead I have . . . An hour of the same fuss
And the same bus and the deserted streets interspersed
With the same transmission from the same politicians
Then once again they show the same train
And still more views on the rolling news
And it's such a pity the Olympic City is being abused
By a handful of men whose own lives are wasted because they wake each day
With hatred in their hearts

So I flick through the channels and I now see panels of experts
Dissecting the day and I must get away from the constant repeats
Of the same old view and I switch to 2 and it's Porridge . . . once more . . .
I'll just try 4 . . . Big Brother . . . reality TV
Yet they don't seem to know that outside their bubble there's so much trouble
And everything is cancelled or a repeat . . . even the date . . .

PART FOUR

BIOGRAPHIES

Sue Ajax-Lewis

Sue spent nearly three decades whizzing around the skies as a trolley dolly, and is now happily retired with a fab part-time job as a guide at Arundel Castle. She is also happily single, with a demanding horse that takes up her spare time (well it gets here out of dusting!).

Alison Batcock

Alison has written poetry since her teenage years and was recently awarded her MA in Creative Writing at Chichester University. The poem and flash fiction featured in this anthology were written as part of that course. She is currently writing her first novel. Alison has been a member of the West Sussex Writers for many years.

Terence Brand

Terry's stories were inspired by his sojourn as temporary clerk and sometime investigator during his 'tour' of Singapore in the early sixties. Singapore was in political ferment and the RAF bods were often called upon to help the 'brown jobs' keep the peace. He even got a medal for his pains! Needless to say, he has souped up the drama occasionally. *A Cushy Number* is the opening tale in the Alfiedog.com series entitled *On the Changi Beat.*

Rose Bray

Rose Bray was born and brought up in the Isle of Man. She trained as a teacher and has lived and worked in the North of England, Switzerland and Sussex. She is married, with a grown-up daughter, a son and two grandchildren.

Rose began writing when she retired from teaching and found it to be absorbing and creative to study and write. She has had several articles, short stories and poems published and won prizes in competitions for both her poems and short stories. She uses stories from her island past and walking by the sea is one of her pleasures which often features in her writing.

Ian C. Black

Ian is the present chair of West Sussex Writers and has written for many years. He mainly writes in play and script format, but occasionally ventures back to the short story form.

Caroline Collingridge

A professional flautist and musicologist, Caroline has taught most of her working life in schools and colleges as well as privately. Having led creative arts therapy courses, she now wants to devote more time to being creative herself. She writes (and performs) her poems and short stories and hopes more of her work will be published in the future.

Suzanne Conboy-Hill

Dr Suzanne Conboy-Hill is a past psychologist, Lascaux Short Fiction, Flash Fiction Chronicles, Pen2Paper, Mash Stories Finalist, and Best of the Net nominee. Her stories have been published by Zouch Magazine, Ether Books, Full of Crow, Fine Linen, and the Lascaux 2014 anthology amongst others. She is editor (and contributor) of *Let Me Tell You a Story*, an anthology of literary fiction and poems by authors of rising international stature whose narrations can be accessed uniquely from the page by QR code. Writing as P. Spencer-Beck, she is also the author of *Not Being First Fish and other diary dramas*. Both are available from Amazon and Lulu. Website: www.conboy-hill.co.uk

Richard Buxton

Richard generally writes historical fiction so his poem Muscovies is a bit of a departure but has special meaning for him. Richard completed an MA in Creative Writing at Chichester University in 2014. His short stories have won the Exeter Story Prize, the Bedford International Writing Competition and the Nivalis Short Story Award.

His first novel *Whirligig* is set in the American Civil War. Current projects include his second book, *The Copper Road*, as well as completing a collection of short stories.

Website: www.richardbuxton.net.

Paul Doran

Paul Doran is a sometimes writer of poetry and short stories - when inspired he seems to have no trouble putting it all together and really enjoys doing it.

Liz Eastwood

Liz is a performance poet who lives, works and performs on the South Coast. She has read her work at numerous venues, including E G Poetry, along with poets such as George Szirtes, Brendan Cleary and Catherine Smith. More recently she was Guest Poet at Tomfoolery in Shoreham and performed in World of Mouth at Cellar Arts Club.

She has won, and been placed, in various poetry and short story competitions. *Book Rape* won the SWAG Poetry competition and was later selected, along with *Ma Fille de la Rue*, for publication in the Brighton Stanza Poets anthology. *One of Those Days* won the 2015 Shoreham Wordfest Poetry Competition and 'starred' at Shoreham Station for a few months.

She has an MSc in Artificial Intelligence and has recently been awarded an MA - with Merit - in Creative Writing at the University of Brighton.

Liz plays and sings - with her husband Derek - in a duo called Bamboozle, runs trail marathons and has an ambition to be the sestina queen of the South.

John Falconer

John Russell Falconer, known as Russell, has been a member of West Sussex Writers for some years and enjoys attending the meetings, meeting other members and discussing their techniques and successes in getting published. Writing has been and still is one of his keen interests. After he retired, he attended Chichester University and gained a BA Hons. Degree in English and Creative Writing - much to his amazement

Patricia Feinberg Stoner

Patricia Feinberg Stoner is a former journalist, advertising copywriter and publicist. Her first book *Paw Prints in the Butter* is a collection of comic verses about cats, sold in aid of Wadars animal rescue. She has just published her second book, *At Home in the Pays d'Oc*, which is the story of two accidental expatriates in the south of France.

Rhona Gorringe

Rhona Gorringe started work in publishing and then left to go travelling. Three years later she turned to teaching and achieved a BA. Redundancy forced a change of direction and she spent twenty five years in the fine art auctioneering world. She belongs to three writers' groups and does admit that they spend more time talking about writing than actually putting the pen to the paper. Despite this she has stories and flash fiction published in anthologies and has been runner up in a couple of competitions. She is trying to get a compilation together and seeking a publisher. Her aim is to, hopefully, provoke some laughter and entertainment for her readers.

Patricia Graham

Patricia has been a member of WSW for over 8 years, but though her attendance has dropped due to health problems. She hasn't been wasting time though. A novel she started approximately ten years ago, under the tutelage of Jan Henley, is finally ready for publishing, entitled *And Let It Harm No One*. She has also been working on a sequel, in between keeping in contact with her 22 grandchildren and 12 great grandchildren. Writing now as Patricia Jack Graham.

Wendy Greene

Wendy Greene joined WSW in 1998 and has served as Secretary and Chairman. In her early career she worked for *Family Circle Magazine* in London, so upon retiring from full-time teaching, she was delighted to become Features Editor for *Essentially Worthing* and, currently, *Caring 4 Sussex Magazine*.

She performs with The Worthing Wordies at the Ardington Hotel and as one of the Roundabout Poets at Worthing Library on about 4 occasions a year.

Seven-seven was written the day after the London tube bombings. Says Wendy, "I was shocked by the numbing effect of the rolling news." She received much applause when it was performed just two weeks later in Worthing town centre where shoppers stopped in their tracks to listen. It appears in her book *You Can't Wrap Your Fish In The Internet*.

Pat Hopper

Pat has been a member of WSW for many years. She writes short stories and novels. She has two grandchildren and now lives in Somerset. She is also a steward at the local museum, which allows her to bore visitors to tears with info garnered from the curator. It's great fun!

Jackie Harvey

Jackie has been a member of WSW since the late 1990s. From 2004, she joined and served on the Committee for a number of years, including the year of the 70th Anthology, *It's an 'Ology*. She's found it great fun, has learnt a lot and met so many wonderful people over the years. Here's to the next ten years!

Alison Hawes

Alison has made her living as a freelance writer for almost twenty years, writing fiction and non-fiction reading books for schools. She has written over 300 titles for 4 to 15 year olds that sell widely in the UK and abroad.

Lyn C. Jennings

Lyn has written poetry on and off for many years, but retirement from Chichester Univeristy as a Senior Lecturer and having time to attend Sarah Higbee's Creative Writing sessions at Northbrook have helped her to refine and restructure her writing. Lyn's main interest is Life Writing and writing about the sea. Lyn has had several poems published in anthologies and has won prizes for her poetry. WSW has been a source of motivation for her because she is in essence a Performance Poet and WSW provides a critical audience which she values.

Audrey Lee

Audrey has always enjoyed writing, painting and performing, but these days chiefly writing. She has published a number of short stories as books, through Amazon Kindle, and used her paintings as illustrations. She lives in Goring and considers herself lucky to have so many artistic and literary friends.

Alexander Medwell

Alexander Medwell is an unpublished poet. He has been writing poetry on-and-off since 1990 and joined West Sussex Writers in 2014. It was the warm reception to his readings at the WSW meetings' open-mic section that finally encouraged Alexander to write more poems and submit them to poetry magazines. It has been a long wait so far.

Laurie Morris

Laurie Morris has been painting, singing or writing something or other for most of her life. Lately, she has returned to the poem as a relatively quick and easy format for creative expression.

Christine Mustchin

Christine lives in Aldwick and Lezzeno, Lake Como. She has written one prize winning and many short-listed competition stories. She published the thriller *From Nemesis Island* (Matador, 2010) and has another completed novel under publisher consideration. She continues to write short stories and is about to complete a memoir of her 93 year old father's wartime experiences.

Janet Rogers

Janet Rogers worked as a news reporter in her twenties, returning to writing when she retired. She has won several national travel writing competitions and her articles have appeared in the UK and Australian press. She is a keen cyclist and swimmer and recently did her first triathlon.

Kathy Schilbach

Kathy has lived and worked in France for the last twenty-five years. She writes both short stories and novels, and has had success with *The People's Friend* and *My Weekly*. Her pen name is Katie Finnemore.

Dave Simpson

Dave Simpson taught at the University of Brighton, School of Education for sixteen years until he retired in 2014. He worked at undergraduate and MA level, and supervised PhD students; he published articles and book chapters on university engagement with its local communities, drama teaching and children's literature. For six years, he ran an innovative education programme in conjunction with a local Brighton school; he also led an Erasmus programme which brought Dutch students to the university and enabled Brighton students to study in Holland. He retired to write the next great university campus novel: cancer intervened, and now he writes poetry and a journal about how he expects to live another day. A poem about his experiences – *This Night before* – was long-listed for the 2016 Canterbury Festival Poetry Prize.

Cherrie Taylor

I have been writing since I was old enough to draw lines in the sand

The sea washed away a great deal of the early work.
Mermaids and fishermen fought over the exquisite prose and poems.
Battles raged. Boats upturned. The sea boiled.
Bidding wars were waged.
Weidensea & Nicolsand won.

They encouraged me to leave the strandline
to pen my prose in a conventional manner
but I mourn the early years…
working to the rhythm of the tides
with the Moon as my guide
holding me steady.

I write everyday.
I surprise myself.
I wobble a lot.

Lela Tredwell

Lela Tredwell is a prize-winning writer of fiction and non-fiction. Her story *The Mart* was published by Fabula Press in Aestas Anthology 2015, awarded Editor's Pick and described as "unflinching, unenjoyable and brilliantly accomplished". Winner of Word Factory's Fables for a Modern World Short Story Competition, her short fiction has also been commended in The Orwell Society's Dystopian Short Story Competition 2014 and longlisted for The Fish Publishing Short Story Prize 2015, while her essays have been published by Thresholds International Short Story Forum. Her most recent non-fiction can be found published with Ernest Journal both imprint and online. In 2013 she was shortlisted for the Bridport Prize and has been awarded a Masters Degree in Creative Writing.

Nina Tucknott

Nina became a member of WSW in 1997 and soon joined the committee in various roles, including being Chair twice. She also helped to run several Day for Writers' conferences in the late '90s and was eventually made an Honorary Member for her services to the club.

Over the years her short stories have featured in numerous anthologies and she has had hundreds of features published both in the UK and abroad. In January 2015 Nina became the Editor of Flora International magazine so her writing continues on a daily basis...

Andrew Westgate

Andrew Westgate is a sixty-three-year-old father of four, grandfather to five. He surfs, practises and teaches Tai Chi and plays guitar. He has been storytelling since the year dot and writing 'formally' since his year out from college in 1977/78. His short stories have been published from time to time in various publications. He had four novels picked up by agents, two went through the publisher's systems only to fall at the final hurdle. He carries on.

Terry Westwood

Terry Westwood has travelled and written diaries for years, trying to capture the essence of these foreign climes. He's written Children & Adult Fantasy, and loves writing all types of poetry and autobiographical incidents. He has a son's wedding coming up and has penned an Ode to be read.

Phil Williams

Phil is a relative newcomer to WSW, having moved to Worthing in 2016. He is a published author of series of novels and grammar guides for students of English. *Of Goats and Gigabytes* is one of his earliest short stories, from many years ago – back before he wrote to market. Website: www.phil-williams.co.uk.

Sandra Wood-Jones

Sandra is a hobby writer and has written occasionally for about seven years, and has been a member of WSW for about two. She enjoys the challenge of flash fiction and short stories. Her ideas come from the mundane; overheard snippets of conversation or ordinary daily life scenes which she then likes to translate into dark and quirky. Sandra has lived in Sussex for thirty years and now resides in Hove.

Lightning Source UK Ltd.
Milton Keynes UK
UKHW041220190521
383993UK00003B/759